Fligh

Helen

AmErica House
Baltimore

First printing

ISBN: 1-58851-843-4
PUBLISHED BY AMERICA HOUSE BOOK
PUBLISHERS
www.publishamerica.com
Baltimore

Printed in the United States of America

Dedication

This book is dedicated to all those who guided me through the creative process, especially my aunt and her sister, without whom none of this would have been possible.

Disclaimer

This is a work of fiction. Any similarities between persons, living or dead, is a coincidence.

Chapter 1

Fiona hated her job. All day long, she stood at a long counter, riffling through other people's personal possessions. As an inspector for the Treasury Department, it was her job to sort the belongings seized under President Gingrich's expanded RICO act. She understood that those involved were criminals, but it made her feel like a voyeur handling all of their things, picking out the "good stuff," and sending the rest out for salvage. The "keepers" were sent to the warehouse, to be stored until the semiannual auction. Fiona couldn't wait to go to the next sale. Recently, they began getting in a more sedate, classier style of goods, not the gold chains and Naga-Hyde stuff the felons usually bought. She guessed they were arresting a higher class of criminal.

She looked over her shoulder at the table behind her, and saw, along with her jacket and purse, a large, gift-wrapped package. It was her grandmother's birthday present, a joint effort between Fiona, and brothers and cousins. Granny's party was tonight; it coincided with her mandatory retirement, and they were having a big family dinner with cake and ice cream. The whole family had squirreled their sugar ration coupons to be able to get the dessert. Damn the "Diet Police" anyway. Things hadn't been the same since that militant nutritionist became Surgeon General.

They all knew that Granny didn't want to let her apartment go back to the Agency, but there was no real way around that. As a widow she wasn't allowed to stay in the big, three bedroom house by herself, and she wasn't about to rent rooms. So she took the money the Agency offered her, and moved into the Singleton Apartments. She always hated it: no room for her own furniture, no pets allowed, she couldn't even paint the walls' anything but off-white. Granny said it reminds her of a room in an asylum for the criminally old. Mostly, she hated the fact that there are only other old women in the apartments. No men allowed. Under the latest policy, all unmarrieds had to remain segregated.

Fiona worried what Granny would think of the gift they got her. A ticket on the new Elder-Shuttle wasn't something she would have bought for herself, but they all were very certain she would like it once she got to thinking about it. Sure it was a long trip, twelve weeks there, then six and a half years on the station, then twelve weeks back. And she could only send or receive discs when the shuttle came in, once a year or so. It had its benefits, though. It was reasonably priced for a seven-year holiday. Granny's pension would be banked, with interest for her, and she would be able to do pretty much as she liked, within the law. And most of all, it was a mixed trip. There would be MEN. Okay, so there's a no fraternization law now, and sex outside of marriage is prohibited under any circumstances for women. But Granny does like to look.

Everybody in the family was excited about her going, too. Well, not Uncle Jimmy; he still didn't know, even though Fiona had to talk to him to get the ticket. Jimmy worked for NASA, passenger division, and had a final say-so over who got tickets. Fiona had told him it was a present for someone at work, and never mentioned Granny's name. Jimmy had problems keeping secrets in the family, and Fiona was afraid he'd blab. He'd find out tonight at her party. Fiona thought it was strange when she called him. He sounded almost hesitant to let them have a ticket. Well, he'd just have to wait till tonight.

Chapter 2

Mary Callahan looked up from her desk, taking a last look around the office where she had worked for the past 15 years. The women there had become a second family, and she'd be sorry to leave them, at least for a while. She was sure she would adjust to not working, and not seeing her friends every day. What she didn't think she could get used too was moving to the facility she called "Geezer Estates." It was bad enough she had to give up her home when her husband died and move into the "asylum," but now she was expected to move into a one room efficiency, not much larger than a jail cell. Getting old was bad enough, but to be forced out of your job at 69 or 70, forced out of your home, forced out of your entire life, all in one month, was beyond comprehension. Now she knew why so many of her older friends had decided to use a "70+." It was called a Euthanasia Drug. Mary knew it was cyanide.

She looked more carefully at the other faces in the office. Most were women around her own age, ready for retirement. The rest were all less than thirty. Since Mr. Newt became president, birth control was almost nonexistent, and premarital sex for women, except those in the government sanctioned brothels, was forbidden. Men who could afford it sought "relief" in the federal red-light district, but for women, there was nothing. No mother of a child less than 12 was allowed to work outside the home. To keep from having 15 children in 14 years, marriage was put off as long as they could hold out, until the biological clock wound down a bit. Even if they were allowed to work, day care was banned. Someone had the bright idea that only a mother could watch a child, and she had to be with the kid 24 hours a day. No wonder so many women drank, or got hooked on prescription drugs. Mary still remembered the song, "Mother's Little Helper." the Stones hit it right on the head.

Mary was thankful she had set aside the money she received from the sale of her house. When the previous administration had abolished Medicare, a lot of the elderly were forced to take the 70+ out of necessity. They couldn't afford to buy medicine and food in the same month. It was one or the other. Then, Gingrich and his Congress full of clones did away with health insurance all together, except for automatic coverage of child birthing expenses. Not only were women forced to give up birth control, but as large families became the norm, infant mortality shot through the roof in most cities. Couples may have six or eight children, but only two or three made it past age five. They'd have to wait and see if any of those survived to adulthood. They were only into the first year of Gingrich's third term, and Mary couldn't wait for him to be a lame duck.

What with his "family values" programs, removal of federal term limits for all posts, forcing half the work force to stay home and be brood mares, and eliminating affordable medical care for the families be forced them to have, Mary thought he was lucky someone didn't take a shot at him the way they did Senator Chelsea Clinton. It was enough to make her resign from the presidential race. Mary always thought it was a shame Chelsea didn't have her mother's balls.

Chapter 3

"Happy Birthday, dear Granny, Happy Birthday to you."Mary looked around the table. Her daughter was there with her husband and their four grown kids. None of the children were married yet. Fiona, the oldest, was only 25, and none of them were ready to become full time parents yet. Jimmy's two kids were there, too, along with his wife, Johnica. Jimmy couldn't get away from his job tonight. Apparently there was a problem with the Shuttle. On the most recent flight a gang of prisoners was being transferred to the Omega prison colony, and there was some difficulty at the departure point. Jimmy couldn't say what trouble, and the TV news wouldn't dare broadcast anything negative about the space program.

Everyone sat at the table waiting for Mary to open her presents. She wondered what was going on: usually there were at least two packages from each person, and a card to go with each. It wasn't that she was mercenary. It was just what she had come to expect.

Her daughter, Erin, handed her a large box, with a card and a huge bow on top. Mary couldn't believe what she found when she opened it: a lovely robe and nightgown. Erin never gave her sensible gifts like nightclothes. She was more apt to give her a glow-in-the-dark Madonna figurine or a musical snow globe that played "It's a Small World" or another equally annoying tune.

Jimmy's wife, Johnica, presented their gift next, this considerably smaller than the one from Erin. It contained a diary and a box of pens. Mary was thrilled. Even though she had used a computer for the last 15 years at work, she still loved to keep her journal every day. And she found writing in long hand so much more personal and satisfying than clicking away on a keyboard.

The six grandchildren stood around, grinning like a

family of 'possums. The anticipation was driving Mary crazy.
"All right, you bunch, What's in the big box? Did you get me a short stripper?"

Under the laughter, Fiona whispered, "Granny, you know you shouldn't be talking like that. What if the Listeners picked that up? What would you do if they took you to the Retraining Center?"

"Come on, Fiona. You know I'd never make it to the Retraining Center. They'd be handing me a 70+ before that black van ever left the parking lot. Do you think I'm that naive? Anyway, you know I was just teasing, don't you?" She said the last a bit louder, though, just in case the Listeners were out there. "So, Fiona love, what's in that huge box your brother's are struggling to heft onto the table?"

"You'll just have to open it and see, Granny," eighteen-year-old Sean said. As Erin's youngest, he was his mother's favorite, and tended to be a little smart-mouthed. Mary still loved him, although at times she wanted to act out her own grandmother's saying and "give him the back of her hand."

"Okay, you lot. Let me get near so I can open it, then," Mary said laughingly as she pushed her way past the grown kids. No matter how old they got, they still put her in mind of a litter of puppies tumbling about. Finally gaining the table, she proceeded to rip the silver and gold paper off the package. Inside, there were about five bushels of shredded paper. Pulling out handfuls of homemade excelsior, Mary wondered if this was Sean's idea of a joke. It seemed like something he'd do. Then she got to the center, and extracted a large gold and silver envelope. In unison, everyone called for to open it.

She could only stare, open mouthed, at the contents. It was a ticket.

Chapter 4

"All right, you hooligans. What's the ticket for? Is this a joke, Sean? If it is, I'm not laughing." Mary was thinking about the forced move she had to make in less than three months, to what was euphemistically called "The Institute." It was warehousing for the elderly, where many of the residents were kept doped on Thorazine and liquid Valium, until they expired of "natural causes." Strange how all the deaths at the Institute seemed to be listed as natural. No one ever committed suicide; no one ever fell and broke a hip. There was never a finding of misadventure. Mary suspected the odor of bitter almonds hung heavily over the place.

"No, Granny," Fiona said. "It's no joke. We all chipped in and got a ticket on the Elder-Shuttle. We knew you'd like it, especially since you didn't want to go to the Institute. We thought this would be perfect. Your pension will be held for you until you get back, and when you do, you'll have enough money from your pension and the house to be able to afford something on your own. You know, nicer than the Institute. If you wanted, you could take the money and move to Ireland. It's allowable for you to permanently leave the country, so long as you establish residence in the country of your ethnicity. We don't want you to go away for a whole seven years, tough."

Sean jumped in. "Remember too, at the Institute, they've got that stupid new policy. It says residents can't have visitors for the first three years, because it might upset them and disrupt the quiet. They seem to think you can't get settled in if you have any enjoyment."

"Now, Mary," Johnica added, "You know Jimmy says the Shuttle is perfectly safe. John Glenn went up in 1989, and people your age and older have been going ever since. I know this is only the second Elder-Shuttle flight, but the first one went off without a hitch. If something was wrong, don't you think Jimmy would tell me?"

"Besides, Granny," Sean said, "All the government agencies, and a lot of private companies are sending their retirees on the Shuttle as a retirement gift. If that company you worked for wasn't so damned cheap, they'd pony up a ticket for you."

Chapter 5

The noise inside the terminal was deafening. There were people milling everywhere, like sheep in a pen. As Mary looked around, all she could see were men and women her own age, each carrying two small bags. Some of them looked ecstatic, while a few looked lost and bewildered. Because of the size of the crowds expected, the agency had canceled all other flights that day, and had ruled only one family member could see a senior off. Sean had volunteered to bring Mary to the aerodrome. Mary still couldn't get over the Gingrich administration's penchant for dredging up archaic words. It seemed as if they wanted the populace to relive the Victorian era, and began by making them speak in Victorian vernacular.

Mary kissed Sean goodbye at the security gate, and turned to wave again after she passed through. Walking down the concourse to the departure gate, she noticed what seemed to be an equal number of men and women. This was something very unusual for age group, as the government tended to keep the sexes segregated religiously. There was also the usual contingent of security personnel. No matter how often she saw them, Mary never became accustomed to the brown shirts with the stylized double S's on the insignia over the Sam Brown belts. Little alarm bells always went off in her head when she saw them; she just never put her finger on the cause.

Reaching the correct area for her departure, Mary stepped into the queue designated for her month of birth. There were supposed to be twenty-four cars on the shuttle-train, with the quarters assigned apparently by dates of birth rather than sex, ethnicity or any of the more prevalent means of segregating the masses. Patiently waiting her turn, Mary looked about, and noticed a sameness on many of the faces. Most of the gathered hordes appeared to be Anglo-Saxon or Nordic, with only a smattering of Hispanics and Orientals. No blacks at all, as the government considered their heritage too diverse to be legitimately traced. Under the Administration's Doctrine of Ethnicity, in order to be in line for any job opening, it was necessary to provide a copy of the family tree. The purer the heritage, the higher rank one could attain. Mary's own family was Irish for at least four generations back. She supposed that was all there was in her family, unless a thorough search turned up some Viking raider in 840 A.D. Sean always said he could be president if he wanted, their lineage was so pure. In return, Mary always responded that Sean couldn't be president, as he was too honest.

As the line wended its way through the serpentine barriers, the presence of so many people, her own age was a surprise. It was rare so many seniors would be allowed to congregate in one place for any length of time. Official policy read that it was to "avoid the spread of airborne pathogens that often accompanies a large portion of the senior population." Mary knew the real reason was to avoid the spread of intelligent dialogue and the exchange of ideas.

Holding her own two bags in her hands, she began to notice what everyone else was carrying. Most, like Mary, had two small bags, one for clothing for the trip, which was limited to what could be carried on board, and a second valise or shoulder bag for medicines, personal care items, and in Mary's case, writing materials and her old CD player and a few cherished discs. CD's went out of style about fifteen years ago, and you had as much chance of buying discs as a 75-rpm record, but Mary refused to give in to the new laser music technology. She thought it took all the feeling and heart out of the tunes.

Everything in the small bags was given a cursory glance by the gate agents and passed back to the passengers. A few had large satchels, the contents of which were being very closely scrutinized by the gate agents. Mary saw more than one senior blink back tears as a memento of the past or a bulky sweater was removed from their bags and sent down the conveyor to "storage." Everyone was told they could reclaim their things when they got home in seven years, as it would be tagged and held for them.

About four places ahead of her, Mary saw one man holding the strangest looking carry on. At first glance, it was a small computer monitor with a handle affixed to the top. However, on closer examination, she bit back a gasp of recognition; it was an old television with a built-in VCR. Video recorders and similar recoding equipment had been recalled twenty years ago, then banned together, when the government decided that home recording of any kind promoted the spread of what they termed pornography. Mary couldn't wait to hear him explain his way out of this, and was glad she was close enough to hear.

The man with the VCR approached the next available gate agent, and Mary strained her ears to listen. The agent, wearing the brown pseudo military uniform of the Security force, read the man's ticket and passport, then began his questioning.

"It says here your name's Johnny Fenster; that right?"

"No," the passenger answered. "It's Gianni Finestre."

"Oh, well I guess that explains it, then. It says here that you're a Dago."

"No, sir. I believe it states I am fifth generation Italian-American, and I have received passage on this shuttle as a retirement bonus from the company for which I worked."

The gate agent sneered at the attractive man.

"Like I said, you're a Dago. Now, what's that thing you're carrying? Some kind of antique like you?"

Mary held her breath, waiting for his reply. Gianni smiled and said, "That's right, it's an antique. According to the guidelines we received, we are allowed to bring aboard

15

personal writing materials. I have used this same Macintosh for the past 25 years. It's all self contained, has voice activation and natural speech capabilities, and as you can see is extremely portable. I only regret I no longer have the battery pack and have to resort to plugging it into the nearest outlet."

Just when it was starting to get interesting, another gate agent down the row called to Mary. She was next. She glanced up at Gianni Finestre as she walked past, and couldn't help smiling when he grinned and winked at her, as if they shared the greatest of secrets. She thought just maybe they did.

Mary stepped up to the desk and presented her papers to the agent. She answered the requisite questions: her name, what was she carrying, and could the agent check her bags. After a quick glance inside, Mary was ready to accept her documents back when a disturbance broke out at the counter, at the other side of Mr. Finestre. Apparently, one of the passengers was trying to bring aboard some item of contraband, and was objecting to its confiscation. As several of the Security Force officers hurried past, Gianni picked up his papers and swept past the officers, as if trying to stay out of their way, and avoid becoming involved in the altercation. Mary was just putting her documents in her bag when he reached her position at the counter. Very smoothly, he reached out, wrapped an arm around her waist and included her in his rush to reach the gate.

Far from a prude, Mary was enjoying the feel of a man's arm around her waist for the first time since her husband died. Bu she knew it couldn't last. Not only didn't she know this man, but they would surely be stopped by the Security Patrol, who were always on the look out for inappropriate public shows of affection.

They passed several security officers who were headed in the other direction, but no one said anything to them. The two of them collapsed, laughing like two teenagers, into chairs in the gate area. Mary looked up at him in amazement. "Did you really manage to pass that TV-VCR combo off as a Mac Compact?"

Gianni grinned at her like a wicked little boy. "Sure did. I just figured it was worth a shot. Whin I saw the fool on duty was young enough to be my grandson, I know it was a go. And I managed to get some tapes through, too. I told him it was what a Mac used for floppies."

His grin was contagious. Mary smiled back at him and said, "It's a shame I'll never be able to see any of them. They'll never let men and women stay anywhere close together. They're terrified that we may engage in something illicit, such as intelligent conversation."

Holding out his hand, Gianni said, "Let me see your ticket."

Mary waited as he compared the two. "Well, look here. We have cabins that not only appear to be next to each other, 17a and 17b. We'll be sharing a bathroom as well, as I presume they are adjoining rooms. I guess the all-knowing powers that be figured out people our ages weren't interested in 'naughty' things anymore."

Mary managed a brief, demure smile before they both broke into gales of laughter.

Chapter 6

"I suppose we should introduce ourselves," Gianni Finestre said. "I'm John Finestre."

Mary gave him a puzzled look. "I clearly heard you tell the kid at the desk, your name was Gianni."

Laughing, he said, "It is. But for years, I've gone by John. Fewer hassles, fewer corrections. Besides, I just enjoyed screwing with the supercilious little bastard's head."

Glancing around quickly, Mary whispered to him. "Please be careful. There may be Listeners here. You're already in trouble if you get caught with the 'Apple.' I wouldn't want you to get into any more."

John smiled at her concern. "Why, nameless lady, one would think, you cared for me already. No worry, though. I was one of the creators of the Listening system. Of course, that was before I knew what the real use would be. It just won't work in a building like this. The ceiling are too high; there's too much background noise and microwave transmitters interfere with the Shuttle's guidance system."

"Oh." She paused for a long time, considering. "I'm Mary Callahan. And you're right. I care about all fools who try their best to get themselves and me into trouble. I can get myself into all kinds of trouble without any help, thank you very much."

"Well, Mary Callahan who cares for all fools, while we wait for the Shuttle to wherever, lets get to know each other a little. We know each other's names; you know what I did for a living. I'm divorced, have been for about seventeen years, before it became illegal. I've got two grown children, both boys. Three grandchildren, all girls. I worked 27 years for the company that makes the Listening system. In my misspent youth, I worked for a variety of companies, mostly factory-type work, while I went to school to learn electronics and design. I retired in May. I was born May 28, 1953, and I'm a Gemini. What about you?"

"Okay, Mr. Gianni "John" Finestre. I'm a widow, have been for the last eleven years. I've got two grown kids, one of each, and a various and sundry assortment of grandchildren. I worked a cutter for an apparel manufacturer, until they designed a computer that could do my job in less than half the time for only a little more than twenty times the cost, and with only a 300 percent higher error and mis cut rate. Maybe later, during this twelve-week flight, you can explain cost-effectiveness to me. Anyway, after I was downsized, I took my severance pay and my federal retraining grants and went back to school to learn data-entry, so I could talk to the computer that took my job. My favorite meal is dessert, and my birthday is November 7, also 1953."

They sat for a while in companionable silence, watching the crowds drift past. After a while, John asked her, "How did you get to come on the Shuttle, Mary? I didn't think your company was giving retirement bonuses of this size."

Laughing ruefully, Mary answered, "Not quite a retirement bonus. For my retirement, they presented me with my last paycheck, gave me a box for my personal belongings, and made me turn in my company ID badge so I couldn't get back on the property. The trip was a gift from the grandchildren. My son, Jimmy, works for the agency in charge of this mess, and they got him to scrounge a ticket. According to my granddaughter, Fiona, Jimmy didn't know the ticket was for me. She told him it was for someone she worked with, whose birthday was in the same month and year as mine. Then Jimmy couldn't make it to my party. So there's a chance he may not know I'm here. But surely his wife told him by now. I doubt they'd keep something like this a secret. There's no need to keep it hush hush now anyway, is there?"

Out of the corner of her eye, Mary saw a tall, red-haired

man in a NASA uniform approach. When he reached the spot where they were seated, he stopped dead and stared directly at Mary.

"Ma! What the holy hell are you doing here? And who is he?"

Rising as sedately as the Queen of England, Mary extended a hand toward John. "Mr. Gianni Finestre, this most respectful and polite man is my son, James Xavier Callahan. Jimmy, say hello to Mr. Finestre."

Wincing at the sound of his hated middle name, just as any small boy would, Jimmy extended his hand to John, who rose to meet him. "Mr. Finestre, I'm sorry to act like such an idiot. But I wasn't expecting to see my mother here with the passengers. So, Ma, what are you doing here? I didn't know your company was giving out bonus tickets."

"If you'd go home to your family once in a while instead of living at the agency, maybe Johnica could have told you. Your kids and Erin's bunch all went in together and bought my ticket. I believe Fiona was the one that talked to you about my passage."

Jimmy looked at her in disbelief. "I'm going to kill that little busy body. I wish she had told me the ticket was for you, Ma. I don't think you ought to go on this trip right now. There's been some trouble on the Shuttle recently. I think it would be best if you stayed home."

"All right, Jimmy, and just where would home be, exactly? The day I left for the Aerodrome, the Housing Authority reassigned my unit. I refuse to go to the Institute. And you know how I feel about that 'panacea for your golden years' known as 70+. I've still got plenty of life in me, thank you very much, and I choose to live it. I refuse to sit in some cloister and vegetate. If I wanted to become a Nun, I wouldn't have married your father. Wake up and smell the coffee, Jimmy. When I first got the ticket, I didn't really want to come, but now I'm here. I do believe I may enjoy myself. I'm meeting new people. For the first time since your father died, I am enjoying the company of a man, without fearing the sex police are going to bust us. Don't you dare come in here with the attitude that you know what's best for me, James Callahan. You seem to forget. I gave birth to you. I blew your snotty nose when you were little. I even wiped your shitty little ass. So don't you even think about telling me what I can and can't do!"

The louder Mary's voice became, the more stricken Jimmy looked. "Ma, you don't understand."

John intervened. "Mr. Callahan, I believe your mother has told you exactly what she thinks. And I think you should let her be. She's all grown up, after all, and knows her own mind." Once again, he placed an arm around Mary's waist, and this time she didn't try to stop him for fear someone would see. "I'll take care of her, Jimmy."

"All right, Mr. Finestre. I'll leave her in your hands. I think that's where she prefers to be, anyway." Jimmy said with a slightly sad smile.

"Call me John, please. And I really will look out for her, I promise. I won't let anything happen to your mother, so long as it's in my power to prevent it."

"That's what worries me, John. There are a lot of things that may not be within your power." Jimmy lowered his voice to a whisper and spoke directly to John. "Just remember, things are not always as they appear. There aren't any monitoring devices in the passengers' rooms, but they are in the common areas and the meeting rooms. Just be extremely careful. She's the only mom I'm likely to have."

Jimmy and John shook hands' Mary hugged her son, and with a final wave, Jimmy returned to his duties as launch coordinator.

22

Chapter 7

John and Mary moved further into the departure area, looking for the proper bay. They were supposed to be in one of the last cars, so it stood to reason that they would be at the end of the concourse.

John apologized for not being able to carry both of their bags, but Mary laughed it off. She told him it wouldn't look right, and besides, what she had weighed less than 25 pounds. Anyway, she had carried it this far, and he had his "Mac" and all that "software" to deal with.

When they arrived at their assigned departure point, they again took seats next to each other, being careful not to touch under the watchful eyes of the security officers stationed by the gate.

As John bent over and carefully placed the TV between his feet, with the screen turned in, he whispered to Mary, "What is so familiar about those uniforms? I know I've seen something really close to those in the past. Just like that new black uniform the president has taken to wearing, the one with all the silver trim. They both create a sort of deja vu."

"I know exactly what you mean. Just like the new national anthem authorized last year. I know the tune is from Handel's Largo, the same one played when the Euro was announced in '97, and I've heard it lots of other times, too. It is easier to sing, but there's something about it that's not exactly right."

John nodded, then stood as if he were stretching. This gave him the opportunity to look around without being too obvious. As he sat down, he said, "There looks to be about 35 people here already. I think there's supposed to be 40 per car. Do yo know yet how this works? I mean, how the cars and the Shuttle get together?"

"Jimmy explained it when the first Shuttle-train went

up. Two cars are launched on one rocket, then they all dock with the shuttle while it orbits. It takes the better part of the day to get them all coupled and underway. Did you know we'll be given a sleeping pill when we take off?"

"I've heard something to that effect. It's supposed to lessen the problems with the G-force, and also cut way back on the motion sickness. Can you imagine a couple hundred geezers all tossing their cookies at the same time? It wouldn't be pretty."

"Well," Mary said, "I, for one, intend to check the pill very carefully before I take it. I don't trust these fools as far as I could throw one of these train cars. The first hint of bitter almond, and all they'll see of me are shoe soles."

"I'll be right behind you. Me and my Apple."

The more they talked, the more Mary liked him. Not only did they understand each other, but John had a way of making her laugh, even when the situation might not have called for it. After all, death by cyanide shouldn't be funny.

Finally, the call came to board in an orderly manner. John found this redundant, as it is not only difficult but highly unwise to be disorderly in the presence of half dozen heavily armed men.

The entire company of seniors made their way down the companion way and into the train car. Once inside, everyone had their tickets in hand, examining doors for the correct compartment numbers. Loudly enough for the Listeners to pickup without any difficulty, when they were in front of 17a, John said, "Here's my room, Mrs. Callahan. Have you found yours yet?"

Mary proceeded a few doors down the passageway before she doubled back. "Oh, here I am. Why look, Mr. Finestre, we're going to be neighbors. I do hope you don't snore."

Keeping his face turned into the door, as he

24

concentrated on inserting his ticket into the security slot above the latch, John glanced sidelong at Mary. "Play your cards right, Mrs. Callahan, and you just may find out."

Mary quickly covered her mouth to keep from laughing out loud. "Mr. Finestre, do you remember a comic that started in the sixties? His name was George Carlin. He said something about suppressed laughter."

"Yes, Mrs. Callahan, I remember." John answered, the absolute picture of innocence. "Why do you ask?"

"It's true, Mr. Finestre." She managed to get her compartment door open and started to step inside. Just before John opened his door, Mary leaned back and whispered, "And you, Mr. Finestre, are a very wicked Man. I like that in a person."

Chapter 8

Instructions had been given prior to boarding to leave the doors to the companionway open until the closing of the main doors was announced. This enabled the flight crew to check on the passengers, and make certain everyone was in their assigned rooms. No trading allowed.

The first thing both Mary and John did was to find the bathroom. They opened the doors on their respective sides and acted surprised when there was a "stranger" in their bath. Mary managed a frightened little gasp, while John fought down more suppressed laughter.

"Why, Mr. Finestre, whatever are you doing in my bathroom?"

"I could very well ask you the same question, Mrs. Callahan. It appears as if we will be sharing facilities. I hope you don't mind."

Still speaking more to the Listeners than to John, Mary said in a slightly haughty tone, "Just make certain you lock both doors when you are in the facility, sir. I shudder to think what I might encounter in my own bathroom. Why, a woman's sensibilities aren't safe, even on a government transport. I just may complain to the Captain. My son works for the Agency, you know. I just may call my Jimmy. He could get this travesty rectified."

John leaned over to her and whispered. "Don't overact, Mary. Keep it up, and they might really move us."

Mary gave him a sheepish grin. "Sorry," she whispered. Then for the Listeners, she said more loudly, "I suppose I could learn to live with this arrangement. It's just for a few weeks, after all. Just make sure you stay on your own side of the door, Mr. Finestre."

"Never fear, Mrs. Callahan. I seldom go where I'm not invited."

Mary leaned up and whispered in his ear, "Play your cards right, Gianni Finestre, and you may get that invitation." With a lascivious grin, John whispered back, "You're a dirty old lady, Mary Callahan. I like that in a person."

Chapter 9

Both John and Mary made a big show of locking the bathroom doors, then proceeded to store their personal belongings. Lockers similar to those on commercial jets were located along one wall in each room, allowing for passenger's clothing and other miscellany to be stored. There were no locks on the doors, but like any mother, Mary knew how to arrange things inside so it would be obvious if anyone tampered with her things. She had done this same thing at Christmas for years, hiding children and grandchildren's presents. Stacking her clothes in the front of the locker shelf in a certain order, she hoped John knew to do the same. She was worried not only about John's privacy, but his security should the existence of his "Mac" be discovered.

About an hour after they boarded, when everything had been stowed away and they'd had time to acquaint themselves with their accommodations, uniformed flight attendants began making their rounds. Each passenger was issued a compression jump suit, and a small medicine cup of pills. Both John and Mary questioned the use of the suit and what medications were being issued.

The attendant explained the suit was to be used for take off only, and it would be reclaimed as soon as their car was linked to the main Shuttle. The suit was made to inflate as the gravity increased, to prevent a sudden drop or rise in blood pressure and subsequent loss of consciousness. The two tablets were a substantial dose of Valium, to induce sleep during lift off. The capsule was Mepregan-Fortis, to help with the sore muscles from the increased G-Force of the launch, with Phenergan added to combat the nausea induced by space travel.

John asked, "Do these work for everyone?"

The attendant smiled at him in that condescending manner many young people have with senior citizens, and spoke to him as if he were just a foolish old man. "It might not stop all the muscle ache and nausea, but with this much Valium in you, I promise, no one will care."

In each room, the attendant pulled out from the wall what appeared to be a seat from an old carnival ride. It had the look of a bucket seat, with a rolled aluminum bar attached to the back and hinged to come overhead to secure across the occupant's lap. It then buckled into a clamp extending from the center front of the seat. When Mary commented it reminded her of her kids' car seat, she earned that same condescending smile.

They were told after they were suited up, an announcement would be forthcoming as to the proper time to take the medication. It took about twenty minutes for the drugs to work, so there wouldn't be much time to walk about. Each passenger was told to get buckled in as soon as they were medicated. An attendant would be round to check on them just prior to lift off to make certain all were well doped and strapped in.

As soon as both rooms were clear, John and Mary met in the bathroom. When John offered to help Mary with her suit, she slapped his hand away, but they both laughed. "I don't need help yet, John," Mary told him. "Maybe later, after we're settled in, we can discuss zippers and buttons and things."

"I'll hold you to that, Mary. Can you believe the attitude of the attendant? She was explaining the effects of Valium to me. She couldn't even pronounce Mepregan correctly. Everyone seems to forget we grew up in the Sixties. What they are passing out as if they were, tiny gold nuggets were once the recreational drug of choice in most high schools."

"Remember, John, the flight crews were all born after 1985. They probably believe the saying 'If you remember the Sixties, you weren't really there.' Just because we were around then don't mean we were active in the drug scene. I mean, I knew a lot of people who did drugs. About 10 percent of my graduating class got hard time for dealing, and about half that many O.D.'d around prom and graduation time. Those were sad days, but I still had a blast. What about you?"

"I experimented a little in high school, not enough to damage any chromosomes or anything. Just enough to know it wasn't my scene. Now alcohol, that's another matter. I enjoy an occasional drink, my recreational drug of choice."

Mary said, "My granddaughter, Fiona, told me liquor is available on board. Red wine is served with dinner for those who take a tipple every now and then. And her brother Sean arranged an honor-bar for me. He's fixed it so there will be a full liquor cabinet in my cabin right after the cars are docked with the Shuttle, and the bill goes to the grand kids. I could even be talked into sharing."

With one last smile, John left Mary to get changed and take care of her personal needs first. All the while he thought how extremely lucky he was to have met her, and to have her as a traveling companion. He just wished they had met ten years ago. Then neither one of them would be on this hell-bound Shuttle. He just hoped they both survived the round trip.

Chapter 10

By the time the sedatives wore off, the Shuttle and all the cars had linked up. Mary wasn't quite certain how it had happened, she just knew they were in forward motion.

The passengers had been instructed to change into the clothing provided to them for the trip, with the exception of certain dinners, when they were encouraged to wear more dressy, or even formal attire. Most of the women had brought a good dress or two along with them, while the men had either a suit or a tuxedo. It reminded Mary of the cruise she took with her husband years ago, except they wouldn't be stopping in Puerto Rico.

The clothes supplied to the passengers were similar to hospital scrubs. Mary and John both saw the similarities to scrubs in that the outfits were unisex. One size fits most, and rather sloppy looking. Mary also thought the colors were a very ugly array, at least what she had been provided. She decided to see if any of the other ladies wonted to trade for something else. Puce was never a good color for her.

John and Mary met in the companionway on their way to the meeting hall. The passengers were told to gather there for dinner and a welcoming speech by the captain. The two of them tried to be nonchalant as they greeted others in the hallway, but John made sure they were never out of each other's sight, and he paid special attention to those around him.

The dining hall was immense. There was seating for all the passengers, with room for the servers to move easily between the tables, as well as the crew and the ever-present security personnel. The tables were set for six, four passengers and two members of the crew. John and Mary's party was rounded out by an assistant purser, one of the senior stewards, a rather mousey looking woman in puce scrubs (Mary believed she had found her trading buddy) and a rather distinguished looking man of military bearing. Mary told John what her son had passed on regarding the first Shuttle. The table assignments were random, but those at the same table were probably assigned cabins near each other, or at the very least in the same car. Unless one asked the purser to change them to another seating assignment, the tables remained the same for the entire trip. The crew members were not always present, however, but they may be on various details throughout the vessel. So, except for designated functions, the seating arrangements were generally for four, passengers only.

The military man at Mary's table introduced himself to the party as Major August Meirhoff. Major Meirhoff had one of those faux English accents often found among the elite in New England. The lady to his left also spoke up, although so quietly Mary had to ask her to repeat her name, Violet Williamson, before she was able to understand what Violet had whispered. Both John and Mary took their turns with introductions, making certain they acted as if they were simply casual acquaintances. Mary thought the Major resembled John Cleese, from "Monty Python's Flying Circus." She also whispered to John when the drinks were being poured that she thought the Major was "kind of cute." John just gave her a look that said he would deal with her later.

As Mary had said, wine was served with their dinner, while dinner itself was standard industrial fare: overcooked, mushy vegetables and mystery meat with salt-free cream gravy, the wine was freely available and poured endlessly by the stewards stationed at each table. For some reason, glasses were never allowed to empty. Most of Mary's group drank sparingly, limiting themselves to one or two glasses. The Major, however, seemed determined to drain the ship's wine reserves the first night out. As he grew more inebriated, he spoke more openly of his military career. He had indeed spent time in England, as well as a good part of his career in

Germany. He talked freely of his time ferreting out Neo-Nazis in the late 1980'a, about the time the Berlin Wall fell. The Major was not only knowledgeable about the skinhead movement in Germany, but of Hitler's Germany as well, as he spent considerable time visiting the archives while there.

After the rather bland meal and equally bland dessert of vanilla custard, the new national anthem was played. As the strains of Handel's Largo began the assembly rose as one, with the exception of the Major, who was by now too inebriated to become upright. The group began to sing along with the recorded music.

America, States united.
Continent joined as one.
One language
One purpose.
All for thee this ballads' sung.

Mary still wondered over the insipid words of the new anthem. In an undertone, she and John could hear the Major singing. But instead of the official works to the national song, what they heard was ***Deutschland, Deutschland, uber alles.***

Exchanging startled glances, John leaned over to Mary and whispered, "Did you ever see 'Casablanca'?" He was very careful that the members of the crew seated at their table didn't overhear.

Mary nodded slightly, and began to sing in her loudest, ball park voice,

Oh say, can you see,
John joined in on the next line.
By the dawn's early light,

Violet joined in, in her own quiet way, then the group

at the next table,

> What so proudly we hailed,
> At the twilight's last gleaming.

Passengers at the other tables joined in gradually. Before the first high note was reached, the entire contingent of passengers was caught up in the fervor, and were united in singing Mr. Key's "Star Spangled Banner." No one realized, other than those at Mary's table, that the small revolt had been to save the drunken Major, they only knew it felt really good.

The security personnel were alarmed by this small uprising and were unsure how to handle it. One of them began to un holster his weapon as the song ended. The Captain laid his hand gently on the guard's arm. "Let them have this one moment, Corporal. God knows. It will be over soon enough for them."

John watched the exchange as the Corporal gave the Captain a stupid grin and snapped the holster over his side arm. As the group regained their seats, John leaned over to Mary slightly and said, "Look at the Captain. Does he look downcast or depressed to you? Maybe I'm reading more into his expression then is really there."

"No, you're not imagining things. He looks genuinely put upon. I just hope it's not the mechanical condition of this ship that has him worried.

Chapter 11

The Captain of the Shuttle was a man in his middle fifties, rather dashing in the black uniform the country now used for almost all its military forces. As John got a good look at the insignia at the Captain's throat, he asked Mary, "Does that medal the Captain's wearing resemble anything you've seen before? I swear, it looks just like the German Flying Cross the Major was talking about earlier."

"Yes," Mary said. "And now that you mention it, isn't his uniform almost identical to the ones Hitler's Luftwaffe wore? John, I'm beginning to have serious doubts about this trip, the country, especially our esteemed president. I mean, all of a sudden up pops the unknown son of the late Speaker of the House, supposedly from a former, unpublicized marriage, conveniently named Newt Gingrich II. No one ever heard of this man before he ran for president. It's like when George W. Bush ran in 1999. A lot of people thought they were voting for his father, then when they found out who he was, it was too late. Any minute now, I expect a giant white rabbit wearing a waistcoat to burst through the door, stare at his pocket watch and announce he's late."

"I agree. We've already got Tweedle Dum and Tweedle Dee guarding the door."

Mary couldn't help but laugh. "John," she asked, "what kinds of side arms are they carrying? During our little insurrection I saw one of the Tweedles start to take it from its holster. I don't think I've ever seen anything like it."

John answered, "Remember the Tazer that was introduced in the 80's? This one is similar, but it doesn't require a wire to penetrate the skin. It's operated by microwaves that cause a kind of nerve and muscle paralysis. It lasts anywhere from a few seconds to an hour. Unless the operator gets carried away, then it can last forever." It was then

John noticed Mary was trying, very poorly, to hold back a fit of giggles. "What did I say that was so funny?"

"When you were a kid, did you ever watch 'The Bullwinkle Show'? They had these two Moon Men who had these ray guns that did the same thing. We were almost 'scrootched'!"

John almost lost control then, himself. "All right, my dear. I stand corrected. We do not have the Tweedle brothers at the door. It is Gidney and Cloyd." Neither of them could hold back any longer, and laughed uproariously. They succeeded in drawing bewildered looks from those surrounding them, who were either not privy to the conversation, or not habitues of Frost Bite Falls, Minnesota.

The Captain stepped up to the podium set up on a small stage at one end of the hall and introduced himself. "Good evening, ladies and gentlemen. For those who haven't met me yet, I'm Marc Kavanagh, Captain of the Elder-Shuttle." Mary was surprised he pronounced it in the Gaelic manner, Kav-en-ach. He continued, "We anticipate our trip will take approximately twelve weeks, give or take, and we hope to arrive without incident. And to the group at the table in the rear," he gestured toward John and Mary. "While we appreciate your rendition of the old hymns, in the future, please confine the sing-alongs to more appropriate times." This was said with a genuine smile that said he knew exactly what they had been about, and he probably would have done the same. "There are numerous activities on board for everyone. All geared to both age and abilities. We don't expect anyone to be doddering old seniors, but we also aren't looking for many Olympic pole vaulters, either. You will find a fully equipped gym, a large heated pool and track on the ship, as well as a general recreation hall, where we hold dances and other group activities for those so inclined.

"Now, I know everyone is wondering what will happen

when we reach our destination. Seven years is an awfully long vacation, especially after one has spent a lifetime working. Once we arrive on Skylab 6, each person here will be assigned a job, if they so choose, and it will be according to your own skills and desires." The Captain seemed to sober as he continued. "No one will be forced to work, of course. It is all strictly voluntary. But is the President's belief that old age can be a kind of prison for the soul, and as he so aptly said, 'Work will make you free.' Ladies and Gentlemen, I bid you a good night, and 'may flights of angels speed thee to thy rest.'"

The Major listed toward Mary as he belched and said, "I wonder if our illustrious president knows the origin of his newest slogan."

Mary looked at the Major with a puzzled expression. As an idea began to take shape, she turned to John and said, "I think you need to invite the Major in for a nightcap before lights out tonight. But for God's sake, don't let him see your Apple or the software."

John gave her a nod. "You know. I had the same thought, exactly."

Flights of Angels

Chapter 12

When dinner was ended, the group at Mary's table began to file in orderly toward the door, exactly as the ship's rules specified. Since their table was located in the rear of the hall, they were the first group out into the companionway. John was careful to stay with Mary, but not close enough to touch, even a casual brush of shoulders. Glancing over his shoulder, John saw the Major walking directly behind them.

"Major, would you care to join me for a nightcap before you retire?" John asked.

"Well, John," the Major answered, nodding toward Mary, "I'd rather join our lovely dinner companion."

Mary pretended to simper, and wished she could summon a blush. What she really wanted to do was slap the lascivious smirk off the drunken Major's face. "Really now, Major. You know that's against the rules. Anyway, I'm not that type of girl." Mary could hear John behind her, trying to hold back a laugh, and straining not to choke in the process. As Mary turned away from the Major, she mouthed to John "George Carlin."

Mary excused herself and hurried down the corridor to her compartment to get things ready. The liquor cabinet Sean had arranged had been delivered, and was well stocked. Mary wondered if they expected her to arrive in a drunken stupor, as they had provided enough alcohol for a Mardi Gras celebration. Taking a bottle of bourbon, glasses and the filled ice bucket from the unit, she hurried through the connecting doors to John's room, and placed them on the desk by the wall. She quickly scanned the room to make certain the "Apple" was safely put away, then returned to the bathroom.

Knowing that men very rarely cared if the bathroom door was closed, she made sure the door on John's side was left standing open, then fixed her door so it was cracked just a fraction of an inch. She positioned a chair behind it, so she could sit and eavesdrop. Just as she was finishing her preparations, she heard John enter his compartment with the Major in tow.

"All right, Major, it appears we have a bottle of Kentucky's finest, and some ice. Let me fix you a glass, and we can sit and discuss things. First, though, I need to get some water for my drink. I never could drink the stuff straight." Stepping into the bathroom, John closed the door behind him. Leaning up against the partially opened door, he whispered, "If you feel uncomfortable sitting there, just knock on the door you're leaning against and holler for us to hold it down. But don't let the Major catch on that you've been listening. If there's anything you don't catch, I'll fill you in later. If it's okay with you, I'll come to your room after I get rid of the lush."

"That's fine. Just be careful how much you drink. I don't want you too tipsy to relate what was said."

Mary could hear the smile in his voice as he said, "Nag, nag, nag. I don't know why I took up with you in the first place."

After John filled his glass with water, he returned to the Major. John found him sitting in the desk chair, working on his second glass of bourbon. John sat on the sofa that doubled as a bed. Stirring the ice in his glass with his finger, he asked nonchalantly, "Major, what exactly did you mean with your comment following the Captain's speech. I may not have caught some of the nuances with all the background noise,"

"You mean his improper use of the Bard of Avon's quote? If I'm not mistaken, that was said to a dead man, kind of an Elizabethan rest in peace."

"No, I was referring to what he said about us being given jobs on the station. I think he said, 'work would make us free' or something like that."

As John watched, the Major shuddered visibly. "When I graduated from college in 1975, I couldn't get a job, what with the economy the way it was at the time. I really didn't want to work in a hamburger joint, which was about the only position open to business majors at the time. So I went in the army. Regular pay, three meals a day, and no worries about housing. Best of all, my Back-Bay mother wasn't crawling up my ass every time I turned around.

"After basic, as we were in the middle of a raging peace, I was stationed in Europe. Back then, if you recall, we were on good terms with most of NATO, and they didn't give us a lot of grief about our nuclear capabilities or troop build up on the Soviet border." The Major paused to take a long drink of his bourbon. "Anyway, while I was stationed in Germany, I got a three-day pass, and went with a few of my buddies on a sightseeing tour. One of the places they took us was a museum in a place called Ravensbruk. There used to be a convent outside the gates, but some of the guards from the old camp turned it into a museum in the late fifties. Do you know what Ravensbruk was, John? Did you ever hear about what went on there?"

John looked puzzled, and said, "The name's familiar, but I can't exactly get a handle on where I heard it before."

"Ravensbruk wasn't the only place like this. There was Treblinka, Sobibor, there were even some privately run camps. But the worst was Auschwitz."

John blanched as the memories came back to him. "What exactly did you see at this camp? I mean, the war had been over for twenty years or more."

"Oh, there weren't any prisoners in the camp. But the camp was still standing. There were long barracks, almost like Quonset huts. The beds inside were huge bunks, built into tiers, each meant to sleep six to ten people per flat, sometimes four or five tiers high. I think the blacks on the old slave ships had it a little better. There, the object was to get as many to the colonies as possible to maximize profits. In the camps, the whole point was to cause death, either by working them to death, or one of the diabolical methods that was devised for expedient extermination. The fewer undesirables, the better for the Reich."

"But what does that have to do with the Captain's little welcome aboard speech?"

"How much attention have you been paying to the new uniforms all the government workers have to wear now? Even the President is wearing a black uniform. Look at the old pictures, if you can find any. The President, the army, even the people who haul the trash all wear the uniform patterned after Hitler's SS. And that little catch phrase, 'Work will make you free,' that was in wrought iron over the gate at Ravensbruk and some of the other camps. *'Arbiett maken frei.'*

Chapter 13

Close to one in the morning, as she lay sleepless on the bed, Mary heard the connecting door to the bathroom open. She whispered, "John, is that you?"

"It's I. Stay where you are; I'll find you."

John made his way to the three-quarter sized bed that doubled as a sofa during the day, and sat on the edge. "After you pounded on the door and told us we were a couple of lushes and to shut the hell up, I had several more revelations from the good Major."

"What exactly did you find out?" Mary asked, sitting up against the wall at the head of the bed. "After I heard the name Auschwitz, I wasn't sure I could stand to listen anymore without saying something. Wasn't that one of the Nazi death camps? You know, now that I think about it, since about the end of 2000, no mention has been made about either Germany's or Japan's role in Wold War II. Then in 2003, the History Channel went off the air, since their programming was 'all WWII, all the time'."

John leaned back against the wall beside Mary and put his shoeless feet up on the bed. It was then she realized he had changed into pajamas and robe. "We have the religious right to thank for that piece of revisionist history. In an effort to bring about 'forgiveness of old wrongs' and 'peace in our times', anything that could bring up old conflict or bad memory was purged from the archives. Remember when we were in school, we learned about the causes of the Civil War, and we had to memorize all the important battles like Gettysburg and First and Second Manassas? Now, the only thing in the text books sounds like something Scarlett O'Hara would say. I believe my grandson called it the 'Late Unpleasantness,' or something like that. All of the old movies about suppression and rebellion against authority, like 'Spartacus', 'Brave Heart', even 'Captain Blood' and 'Robin Hood' has been destroyed. The censors have taken away everything that might show things can be changed, and blind acceptance is not always a good thing."

"You know, I always thought those old films had just fallen out of favor, or maybe it was because they contained love stories and some implied sexuality that they were banned. I never thought about what the real agenda might have been. What else did you find out?"

"I'm afraid it gets worse," John said as he reached over and took her hand. "The Major was sent here by special order of the military. He had to receive special dispensation, as he is only second generation native born."

"What was all that talk about his 'Back Bay Mama,' then? Was it just another fabrication of the establishment to infiltrate our circles?"

"No, his mother's family are really Boston Brahmins. However, his father's family were refugees from the Nazis during the Second World War. His last name is Meirhoff, but not the Baltimore Meirhoff's. That's why he introduces himself mostly by his rank, and why he still wears regimentals as his formal attire. He's retired, so he is entitled. It just seems a bit unusual, until you learn the circumstances. After he went to visit some of the camps in Germany, he went back stateside, and was put in charge of a fact-finding mission, about what actually went on there. It seems not all the camps were like Auschwitz. Oh, I don't mean there were good places, and the people were sent there with the intention that they should be worked to death. But aside from the extermination camps, there were labor camps. They sewed uniforms for the German troops. One camp, made lace for the officers' wives. At Ravensbruk, they had some watchmakers and other skilled workers there. That in itself was unusual, as it was primarily a woman's camp."

"Don't tell me your one of those chauvinists who thinks women can only run a sewing machine and make babies!"

"I didn't say that. It's just that in 1941, it was unusual for a woman to be skilled in that type of work. Anyway, there were mostly Jewish women who grew up helping in the family trades, and learned their skill from the cradle. They made weaponry at Ravensbruk, including bomb sights for the Luftwaffe."

"All right. But I don't see what that has to do with the Major. I can see how it would upset him. He probably lost family during the Holocaust. That would unbalance anyone who was thrown back into it the way he was."

John squeezed the hand he was holding and smiled in the dark when Mary didn't pull away. "As I said, he was ordered to prepare a report about what went on in the camps. Later, just recently as a matter of fact, he found out his report has been put into action."

Mary was suddenly uneasy, even more so than before. She sat up straighter and reached around John to turn on the bedside lamp. "I want to look at your face when you tell me this." She became doubly alarmed when she saw tears gathering in his eyes. "John, what did you learn? Please tell me; I think I deserve to know the truth."

John took a deep breath, cleared his throat and reached for Mary's hand again, realizing he needed both her comfort and her strength at that moment. "After the Major's report was finished, it was filed away, and he forgot about it, until he saw the plans of the Elder-Shuttle at the Pentagon. He threatened to go to the media with the story when it was first planned, about seven years ago, but they silenced him by posting him to some Godforsaken location and making vile threats about the safety of his family. Joel--by the way, that's Major Meirhoff's given name--explained exactly why the Captain made that statement during his speech."

47

"You mean, 'Work will make you free'?"

"No, not that one, about the 'flights of angels.' I thought it was just an improper use of Shakespeare at the time. Mary, do you know what the name of this shuttle is? And do you know for certain where we're supposed to be going?"

"I thought it was just the Elder-Shuttle, and was told we'd be going to a space station for the next seven years. I guess that's not true though, is it?"

John took a deep breath, as if gathering courage. "This shuttle is named the Dark Angel. The space station is really a man-made asteroid in permanent orbit just beyond Earth's moon, with a bio-dome and self-sustaining ecosystem. It's possible for people to live their entire lives there, without any contact with the outside, if they so choose. This is where many of the crops for the U.S. are grown now, since the government closed our borders and all communication outside the country is forbidden. There is a shipment made once a month from the produce and aquiculture in the hydroponic greenhouses. According to Joel, we are being sent there as a form of forced labor. As we are not allowed to have contact with our families, except by an annual computer disk sent through the mail, they will have no way of knowing what our real purpose will be, as our letters will be ghost written for us. They will also not know when they receive the letter stating we really enjoyed our time on the station, and we aren't coming back, that it means we have either been worked to death, or used for an even more insidious purpose. I think that's why your son, Jimmy couldn't say anything about the true mission; he would just try to keep you from going."

"But what's more insidious than being worked to death? What do they intend for us to do? I, for one, am too old to become a government hooker, and so are you. I can't believe watching tomatoes grow in water and feeding fish once or twice a day would be anything too strenuous."

"No, Joel told me they have factories set up, too. Almost all of the passengers have some industrial experience. The equivalent of sweat shops are open out there, sewing factories to make cheap clothes and shoed for the masses back home. We can't get our inexpensive goods from third world countries anymore, so Mr. Newt decided to establish his own, from his own citizenry, using the lowest class of all. Us! And remember, warm bodies are a renewable commodity. They'll work us till we're ready to drop, and no one will say a word, because the elderly are like sheep. We follow orders, for the most part, and rarely make waves."

"I suppose it's too late to change our minds and go home?"

"I'm afraid we can never go back home, my love. That's why Jimmy was so aghast when he saw you. What we need to understand is the real reason we have been sent here to die. The Major told me the project is called the Elder Solution, like Hitler's Final Solution. They expect us to roll over and die on command, but I don't favor that idea, myself."

"I agree. Since we turned fifty, the doctors have been pumping us full of various hormones so we don't age. For a while around the same time insurance companies were paying for plastic surgery, as enhancing ones' self esteem was believed essential to good mental health. Almost everyone had something lifted, fluffed or enlarged. We don't die at sixty like our great-grandparents, or at eighty like our parents. But now that we live into our hundreds, they don't know what to do with us."

"It seems they have found a use for us after all. Keep in mind the strict rule on ethnic purity, so there is limited genetic interference. After they work us until we can't do much more than breath unaided, they bring the insidious part into play. It seems there is a medical facility in the bio-dome as well, where other things are harvested. We are to be organ

49

farms for the rich and famous. That's why they gave the place that horrible name."

Mary just couldn't take it all in at once. She laid her head over on John's shoulder and asked, "All right, John, you've told me the worst of it, I think. What did they name this little piece of paradise where we've been condemned?"

"Think about it. We're not expected to return. They named the shuttle after an angel, and the religious right has pretty much taken control of things. The name's almost funny, since the film by the same name was a colossal flop, and the group using it all checked out in a mass suicide. They call it "Heaven's Gate.""

Chapter 14

Mary stared at John in disbelief. "John, you can't really be serious about this. Are we supposed to believe our own government would treat us like the Bosnians in Kosova or the Jews in Nazi Germany? I never would have thought it possible something could happen in our country"

"Many, I think it ceased to be 'our country' about 10 years ago. When was the last time the public had any say in public policy? The government has taken control away from all but the highest offices in Washington. The halls of Congress are filled with drones, whose only job is to do the will of the administration."

"Do you think it's the same world wide? I mean, the senior citizens being kept alive in Europe and Asia as walking organ banks?"

"I don't think so, but there's really no way for us to know. Since our borders were closed five years ago, no news from the outside can get in, and no one out there knows what goes on within. It's like living inside a giant bubble, with no escape."

Mary sighed and lay back against the wall again. "I'm almost afraid to ask. Did you learn anything else from Joel?"

John squeezed Mary's hand once more. "I found out I'd rather not be alone with him again?"

"Oh, no," Mary laughed lightly. "I didn't think the Major swung that way. What about all that talk in the hallway?"

"That's what it was: talk. The real reason Joel went in the military was he was looking for a few good men. That's also the reason he tried so hard to get away from mama. She kept pressuring him to continue the family dynasty, and all he wanted to do was join the Village People."

"You know, John, it's sad, really. Here's a man making

a career out of the army, who had to hide his sexual preferences for his entire life for fear it would get him imprisoned. I know for a very brief while it was considered okay, and legalized. But then the powers that be became the powers that were, and those considered sexual deviants were rounded up and sent to the Arizona Dessert. Will there ever be any justice again?"

"Was there ever any justice? For some, there was; you know that. But there have always been groups singled out for discrimination. Sometimes it's blacks, or the Irish, or Jews or women. I guess this time it's our turn. This is one time I wish someone had cut in line ahead of me."

Mary reached over to turn out the light, then snuggled down into the bed. She turned toward John. "Well, since there doesn't seem to be anything we can do to fix the situation, especially at two in the morning. I vote we get some sleep."

John said, "Well, I guess I'll say 'Goodnight, 'then," and started to get up.

Mary laid a hand on his arm. "You know, you don't have to, if you don't want to."

"Don't have to what?" John asked, playing dumb.

"You don't have to leave."

"Are you absolutely certain? Aren't you afraid we might be caught in a compromising position?"

"I don't think these idiots they've set to watch us think you're up to a compromise. Besides, if this is going to be my last trip anywhere, I plan to spend it doing what I like best. My daughter gave me this pretty new nightgown, and I don't want to wear it out too fast. After all, it has to last at least the next six years, or until I've outlived my usefulness."

John climbed back into the bed, but this time slid under the covers. "Well, madam, if it's a compromise you really want, I'll do my best to oblige. But I don't know if I can keep it up for the entire trip."

Mary laughed, a slightly dirty laugh. "That's all right,

John. So long as you keep it up when we're alone, that's enough for me."

Chapter 15

About seven in the morning, a knock sounded on John's door. Scrambling to recover his pajamas and robe, he hurried through the connecting doors, closing Mary's completely, but leaving his ajar, as if he was just coming out. Mary could hear nothing, but made it a point to don her gown and robe, just in case. In a few short minutes, there was a knock at Mary's door, as well. One of the ship's stewards was there with a message that the Captain wanted to see both Ms. Callahan and Mr. Finestre in his office immediately after they had breakfasted.

After Mary closed the door, she opened the bathroom door, and joined John in his cabin. "What do you think that's all about? Do you think we've been busted already?"

John put his arms around her comfortingly. "God, I hope not. With my luck they'll make me share facilities with Joel. And did you notice Violet looking at you at supper last night? I wouldn't be surprised to learn she had a few skeletons in her closet as well."

"Well, if it's not that, why does he want to see us?"

John shrugged, and began to gather some clothing for the day from the chest bolted at the foot of his bed. "Probably its regarding our little insurrection of last night. I don't think it went over too well with the ship's company, especially Gidney and Cloyd. I've got a feeling those two went to the Captain for permission to scrootch us anyway."

Mary watched him move about the room. "I guess it's not worth worrying about anyway. Worst case scenario. They get to scrootch us permanently. How about we get showered and changed, and do something about breakfast?" Mary walked back into the bathroom, and John followed, closing his connecting door behind him.

John leered at her. "Is that an illicit invitation I hear? If it is, the answer is an unequivocal 'yes'!"

"No, you dirty old man," Mary laughed. "That was NOT an invitation. I may have just spent a most enjoyable night with you, but I do not think we can both fit into that postage stamp sized shower stall. Who did they build those things for, anyway? There's hardly room for one person in there, let alone two, with something other than cleanliness on their mind. And I firmly believe if I got you in the shower, washing would be the last thing we would do."

Mary heard John call to her as she closed her door, "And you had the nerve to call me a dirty old man, Ms. Callahan." She just smiled.

After they were both showered and dressed in the scrublike uniforms provided for the trip, they proceeded with the rest of the passengers to the diningroom for breakfast. They were in the second seating for the meal, and arrived about halfway through the service. They made their way through the dining room to the buffet, and picked up their plates. Unlike supper, this was a rather imaginative meal, with fresh fruit, juices and at least three meats, and vegetarian entrees on request. Mary told John she supposed this was to keep them healthy for the trip, so they didn't come down with scurvy or beriberi. John told her to hush.

They joined Joel and Violet at their assigned table. As they ate, Mary looked up to see both Violet and the Major studying her. "Is anything wrong?" She asked. "Do I have spinach between my teeth or something?"

Joel and Violet exchanged glances. Violet said quietly, staring at her plate, "I saw the steward at your door this morning. I wondered if anything was wrong."

Mary swallowed the piece of peach she had just put in her mouth, trying had not to choke. She took a sip of water, then answered, "No, I don't think anything's wrong. He just brought me a message, that's all. I'm certain it's nothing really important."

"No, my dear," Joel volunteered "I'm sure nothing's wrong. Probably just usual ship's business."

As they were finishing the last of their meal, the two security officers John had dubbed Gidney and Cloyd appeared at John and Mary's sides. Cloyd, the one with the mustache, leaned down to John and said, "Mr. Finestre, the Captain will see you and Ms. Callahan now. Come with us, please."

As they left the table, they heard Joel tell Violet, "At least those two don't have their weapons drawn. That's one good sign."

John thought so, too. He just wished he knew what this was all about.

Chapter 16

Mary and John preceded Gidney and Cloyd down the long corridor and across the transom into the next car, where the officer's quarters as well as the Captain's office were located. They were directed to stop at the last door on the right, and Cloyd reached between them and knocked soundly on the door, without waiting for an answer from within, Cloyd then pushed the door open, and with a slight pressure on John's shoulder, guided them inside. Mary and John were directed to sit on the sofa along one wall, and told the Captain would be with them in a few minutes.

John thanked them for their trouble, and waited for them to leave. Turning toward Mary, he simply glanced up into the corners of the room, to show her he thought they were being observed, then rubbed his ear, to let her know the Listeners may be active as well.

Mary said, all innocence, "What do you think this is about? This has me worried. I hope nothing's wrong at home. You know, that's always the first thing a mother imagines, that something has happened to one of her children."

John patted her hand in the manner of a concerned stranger.

"I'm sure there's nothing wrong. It's probably just ship's policy or something. Or maybe there was a discrepancy in one of our tickets, and we're to be moved to other quarters."

After a few minutes of uncomfortable silence, the door at the rear of the room opened, and Captain Kavanagh entered. Walking to where John and Mary were sitting, he said, "Ms. Callahan, Mr. Finestre, I'm glad you decided to join me. I was worried you might decide you'd rather not. I'm afraid we might have had a scene on our hands, if that was the case."

"What exactly is this about, Captain?" John asked.

"We weren't quit finished breakfast, and those two big

bruisers came and took us out of the dining room in front of everyone. And as you can see, Ms. Callahan is worried half to death something is wrong. What's going on?"

"I wanted to have a word with you two before we took any other action. No, Mr. Finestre, let me finish. I received a communication this morning from NASA. There are several people on this trip who need to be shuttled back home as soon as possible. One is a steward in the twelfth car, who had a death in the family soon after we took off. Unfortunately, you two are the others who will be rotated home as soon as we reach Skylab 6."

"Captain, " Mary spoke up, "what's going on? I don't think I understand."

"Ms. Callahan, there appears to be some difficulty with both yours and Mr. Finestre's heritage. While normally it would not present any problems, in order to be considered for this mission, it was required that participants have verifiable ethnic lineage for at least three generations in our country, and at least 100 years prior to arrival in the New World. There appears to have been a slip up when your respective files were prepared. Ms. Callahan, it seems as if there is some Scandinavian blood mixed in with the Celtic. An unfortunate event, to say the least. And Mr. Finestre, there has been a finding that one of your Northern Italian forebears mingled with a Basque woman. Also, an unfortunate event. This obviously makes you both unsuitable for our mission, and will require that you be transported immediately upon arrival to the space station. In the mean time, I would prefer if you were separated from the general ship's population, and request that you both move your things into the holding area."

John couldn't help asking, "Captain, this 'holding area', is it anything like we used to call the brig when I was younger. If it is, I don't think that will really be necessary, especially for Ms. Callahan."

Chuckling, the Captain said, "No, Mr. Finestre, it's not the brig. Our holding area is also set aside for visiting VIPs and others who need to be sequestered. It has a large common area, two bedrooms and two full bathrooms. It resembles a large hotel suite. Your meals will be served to you there, and you may enjoy full run of the ship, so long as you are escorted either by a steward or a member of the ship's security officers,"

John rose and offered his hand to the Captain. "Captain Kavanagh, I think that would suit us very nicely. If one of the ship's stewards is present, may we entertain a guest or two in our suite as well?"

"So long as there is someone else present, I don't see were that would be a problem. Why do you ask?"

John took Mary's elbow as if to assist her from the chair. "Ms. Callahan, would you excuse us for just a few minutes? I'd like to have a few words with Captain Kavanagh privately."

Mary looked at John as if he had just sprouted an extra set of eyes. "Of course, Mr. Finestre. I believe I'll give one of those nice young men at the door escort me to my state room. If you would excuse me, gentlemen." Mary swept from the room as regal as the Scottish queen for whom she had been named. She just hoped her head wasn't going to be on the block as her namesake's had been.

As soon as she had closed the door behind her, John turned to the Captain. "Captain Kavanagh, have you a minister on board, someone who is licensed to perform marriage ceremonies?"

Chapter 17

Mary was busily getting her meager belongings together, when she heard the door to John's room open and close. Going to the connecting bathroom, she opened the door on his side and called softly to him. John met her with an embrace that ended in a long-awaited kiss.

"John, what was so important for you and Captain Kavanagh to discuss that I couldn't hear? Just so you know, I am no shrinking violet who must be protected from any little difficulty. I thought we had already worked that out."

John took her hand and led her back into her own room. He motioned for her to sit on the sofa while he took the chair, after first positioning it so they were knee to knee. "What I needed to speak to Captain Kavanagh about did concern both of us. But I didn't want to get your hopes up prematurely."

"John, what is going on?! I do not like secrets and being kept in the dark. This is not a Christmas present that needs to be hidden away until December. We're talking about our lives!"

He slid forward on his seat, and took both her hands in his. "I had to go over some things with the Captain before I talked to you. But now that everything has been worked out, I need to ask you a very important question. Ms. Callahan, will you do me the honor of becoming Mrs. Finestre?"

Mary stared at him, open-mouthed. "John, what the hell are you talking about? We're in danger of being eliminated and you're asking stupid, rhetorical questions. Now tell me the truth. What is going on?"

"Mary, my love, I am neither joking nor am I speaking in rhetoric. I want very much to marry you, as soon as possible. That was my reason for speaking to the Captain. As soon as I have your answer, we are to finish getting our things together and retire to our new suite. He will meet us there to work out the arrangements, that is, if your answer is 'yes'."

Mary lunged forward and grabbed John about the neck, almost tumbling both of them onto the floor in the process. John chuckled and said, "does that mean 'yes'?"

When Mary had finally gotten over the complete shock, she released him. Smiling and wiping away a stray tear, she said, "Yes, Mr. Finestre, I would be deeply honored to become your wife. So long as you don't expect me to have five or six children. You'll just have to settle for step kids and grand kids. Eventually, we may even have some great-grands. Would that suit?"

John pulled her to her feet. Giving her one last squeeze, he said, "That would suit me very nicely, indeed. Now then, get your things together. I need to pack my Mac so it's not so obvious, then we can go. The Captain said he will meet us in our new digs in about an hour, and that was twenty minutes ago. We'd better get going."

John was putting away his clothing in his bag when Mary came in with one of her carry-on bags. "Will your Mac fit into this? I can get all my stuff into one bag, and I thought this might help."

"Immensely. Hold it open for me, and I'll fit the little devil down inside."

"John, do you have anything we can pad around it, so it doesn't look quite so square? Right now, it looks like a TV in a suitcase."

"How about my bathrobe? I'll cram it down around the edges. If anyone looks inside, they'll just think I'm a slob."

"All right, Mr. Finestre. I'm ready. You're ready. Shall we go on to our new accommodations?"

"Yes, Ms. Callahan," John said, taking her hand, "I think we should."

Shouldering the bag with the contraband TV, John picked up his other bag while Mary took up her now single carry-on. As they reached the door, Mary pulled back. "John, I don't think it's a good idea for us to leave together. It might make things look bad. It's bad enough you had to go and ask for permission to get married." When John started to protest, Mary held up a hand to stop him. "You know I didn't mean it that way. I just want it to look 'regular' when we leave here."

"If that's what you want, Mary. I'll go out first and wait for you in the hall. But that doesn't mean I have to like it."

Mary reached up and gave him one last kiss before going back through the door connecting the two rooms. John went out into the hall and leaned on the wall. "I don't suppose Ms. Callahan has come out yet, has she?" he said to one of the guards. "I swear, I think men still spend half their lives waiting for women."

The Tweedle brothers exchanged glances and sniggered to each other, shifting their weapons lightly in the holster, as if they expected John to try and rush one of them at any minute. At this point, Mary opened the door to her cabin and emerged into the hall. "Well, what are you waiting for," she said to the three men. "Here I rush to get everything together in just a few minutes, and you lot are lounging about as if we had all day. I never will understand men."

Mary and John fell in side by side, as the Tweedles took up point and drag positions. As they went down the corridor to the connecting transom, Mary took one last look around. "I suppose we just follow this gentleman to our new quarters?"

Finally, the Tweedle with the mustache, the one Mary dubbed Cloyd, spoke up. "Yes ma'am. Just keep following Dakota. We've got two cars to go though before we et to the one you'll be staying in."

"Dakota," Mary repeated. "Is that the other young man's name? And what's yours? I hope you don't think we're too forward. It's just nice to know who will be around in the future."

"Yes, Ma'am, he's Dakota. My name's Austin. I believe we've been assigned to you and Mr. Finestre for the duration of the trip. The two of us, and two other teams are scheduled to take shifts, to make certain you're undisturbed."

John shot Mary a sidelong glance. His only comment was, "Un-huh."

When they reached the end of the car housing the officers' quarters, they came to one last door, at the end of the car where one would expect the transom exit to be. Dakota pushed it open, and ushered them into a spacious room, with four doors leading to what Mary supposed were the other bedrooms and bathrooms. In the main room, she found a settee, two chairs and a low table, suitable for playing a hand of cards or holding a small, portable TV. There were also numerous electrical outlets throughout the room. When Mary questioned Austin about the availability of power, he volunteered, "Many of the VIPS who stay in this suite need to access information units, what you would probably call 'P.C.'s'. It makes it simpler to provide them a place to plug in rather than provide rechargeable solar pacs. Now, then, I think we should leave you two to get unpacked, if that's all right."

"Yes, that will be fine," Mary said, smiling. "You two just run along and have fun. We old folks will settle in and I guess we'll see you later."

After the two guards closed the door behind them, John and Mary collapsed on the settee. "God, Mary, you sounded just like June Cleaver. 'Wally, you and the Beave play nicely with Lumpy. I'll call you in time for dinner.' How did you do that with a straight face?"

Mary gave him her most beatific smile. "Well, Dakota and Austin were playing Eddie Haskell, why shouldn't I be June?"

John leaned over to give her a small kiss on the cheek. "You can be June, so long as I get to be Ward. But I'm warning you now, I will not button the top button on my pajamas, and no twin beds."

"Fine with me. Speaking of twin beds, what is this about marrying? How did you convince the Captain, and who is going to do the ceremony?"

"I told Captain Kavanagh I believed I had already compromised you when I walked in on you in the shower. He believed me, as I don't think he grasped the full meaning and possibilities of 'compromise.' He is providing us with the ship's chaplain. The Captain is going to stand as best man, and I hope you don't mind, but Major Joel Augustus Meirhoff is going to give the bride away. He should be sober enough by now. Would you like Violet to be a Matron of Honor?"

"No, I don't think that will be necessary. I believe the Major can fill that roll as well, don't you?"

Chapter 18

John and Mary took time to dress in their more formal attire. Mary in the dress she bought for dinners and John in his suit. By the time they were finished, the Captain and Joel had arrived, along with a distinguished, somber looking man wearing the ship's uniform with a cross emblem on the collar of his blouse.

Captain Kavanagh introduced Lieutenant McKendree as the ship's chaplain, who had consented to perform the ceremony at the Captain's request.

The chaplain said, "I understand I've been ordered to perform this wedding, but I want it on the record I believe it is a travesty. Marriage is a divine institution intended strictly for the procreation of children. At your age, it's obvious you can't even consummate this union. And given the bride's age, I don't think she'd be interested anyway. I'm only here at the Captain's insistence."

"Lieutenant, I believe you've made yourself perfectly clear," the Captain said, firmly. "You and I have already had this conversation, if you cannot carry out my orders in a timely manner, I will see you expelled from NASA upon our return to our home base. After which I will personally make certain you never hold a position of authority in any congregation other than a bunch of snake handlers in Appalachia. Do I make myself clear?"

Before the Chaplain could form a response, John approached him. "Captain Kavanagh, may I say something to the Lieutenant?"

"Yes, of course, Mr. Finestre, be my guest," the Captain said with a small, knowing smile.

"Lieutenant McKendree," John began, "If you do not want to perform this ceremony, you do not have to. Just remember, our sins will be on your soul."

"What sins do you mean, sir?" the Chaplain asked grimly.

"Why, the sin of lust, and fornication, of course. You don't think I want to marry this fine lady just for the companionship, do you? If I wanted a buddy, I'd have a cat. I want someone in my bed, whose feet I can keep warm on cold nights. I want a woman I can make love to. Yes, don't look so shocked. Even us old farts have carnal urges. You're about 30, I'd say. And I bet your pecker quit working last year, about the time you decided everyone had to be celibate that wasn't married. You're wife has probably already dropped three or four kids, and after the last one, she threatened you with castration if you touched her again, didn't she? You're not getting any, ergo, no one else can, either. You know, that's the best thing about being our age, Lieutenant, you still have urges, you can still act on those urges, but the consequences do not include unplanned pregnancies."

Mary moved beside John and wrapped an arm around his waist. She looked up at John and smiled, "John, I don't think I want to get married now. I believe I would rather live in sin with you than allow this self-righteous little twit perform a service so personal for us."

Deciding it was time to really shock the "little twit" a little more, John wrapped his arms around his fiancé and kissed her soundly, VERY soundly, all for the benefit of the Chaplain. when they broke apart, gasping for breath, Mary was giggling like a highschool girl. John turned to the Chaplain. "Lieutenant McKendree, gentlemen. I think you should leave us alone now. It's obvious Ms. Callahan has other plans for me, and at the moment they do not include observers. So, unless you are into voyeurism, I suggest you all be elsewhere."

The Captain cleared his throat. "Mr. Finestre, I believe Lieutenant McKendree will do his sworn duty at this time, without any further sermonizing and proselytizing. He knows

I do not allow that aboard my vessel, and he will be duly reprimanded. Now then, Lieutenant, you may continue with the wedding, as we are all assembled, and the bride and groom are obviously ready."

Mary said, "Thank you, Captain Kavanagh. If we have a son, I want to name him Marc, after you."

While Captain Kavanagh, John and Mary were still laughing, the Major was admitted by Austin. He congratulated John and Mary, and shook the Captain's hand. He starred at the Captain intently, as if trying to place his face. "Captain Kavanagh, was your father in the Air Force, assigned to the European command in the late 1990's?"

"Why, yes, as a matter of fact, he was. Do I know you, sir?"

"You should," Joel answered. "Do you remember your dad bringing home a bachelor officer for Christmas one year while you all were stationed in Berlin? You would have been around eight or nine years old, and you had a sister named Colleen, I believe, who was three years older. Your mother's name was Sylvia, and your father was John Francis Kavanagh, at that time I think we were both Captains."

The Captain stepped forward and grabbed the Major in a bear hug. "Uncle Joel!" he cried. "You were the last person I expected to see onboard. I never put Augustus Meirhoff and my Uncle Joel together. I don't think I ever knew your last name."

"How on earth did you get here is the better question, Marc. But, I think we can discuss that after we stand up for these good people, don't you?"

The Chaplain interrupted the two men. "Captain, I know you ordered me to perform this ceremony, but I personally believe it to be precipitous. Why, it was my understanding they just met. And you know as well as I that marriages formed in haste rarely if ever last."

71

Mary couldn't hold back. "Lieutenant McKendree, I have already stated my opinion of you. Please don't give me any more fuel for the fire. Besides, when one reaches our age, one may not have years and years to get to know the other person. Why, our marriage may only last until we get to our destination. One of us may drop dead tomorrow, for all we know. And we would like to make the best of our remaining time together."

Finally, the Chaplain relented. Gathering the wedding party together, he hastily read through the vows, as if he had taken Mary's words about dropping dead to heart. When the words, "I now pronounce you Husband and Wife" were intoned, John grabbed Mary and kissed her in a way meant to dispel any notion the Lieutenant may have had about their lack of sexuality.

While the rest of the wedding party applauded, they went on kissing until they finally came up for air. Mary gasped and slapped at his shoulder playfully. Laughing, John said, "All right, gentlemen, you've done your duty; now get out. The lady and I would like to be alone if you don't mind."

The Captain joined in the laughter. "Not so fast, Mr. Finestre. You invited us here to take part in a wedding, and I believe a reception usually follows." The Captain opened the door to the passageway, and admitted a trio of stewards, each pushing trolleys bearing an assortment of breads, fruit, cheeses and meats.

The last of the line contained a large, decorated cake. "I hope you'll forgive the simplicity of the fare, but you have to admit, this was rather short notice. Fortunately, we had a cake on board ear-marked for someone's birthday, but I managed to commandeer it for the celebration today. And I also managed to procure this." Reaching under the cloth on the trolley containing the cake, Captain Kavanagh came up with a Jeroboam of Champagne. "This I keep on hand for special occasions such as this."

"Captain," the Chaplain said, disdainfully, "I've already made it plain how I felt about participating in this farce of a wedding ceremony. I will not condone any type of celebration that involves both sugar and alcohol. That is beyond the pale, and I cannot countenance this ship's captain being involved in such, either."

John took the Chaplain by the elbow and ushered him to the door. "That's quite all right, Chaplain, we wouldn't want to offend your tender sensibilities." They reached the door, and John opened it. Giving the Lieutenant a shove out of the room and slamming the door shut, John called through the closed panel, "And, besides, you little pip-squeak, who said I wanted you at my party, anyway?"

As he turned away from the door, John heard the "pop" of the champagne bottle. The Major held out two glasses in each hand for the Captain to fill. Handing them around, he held his own glass aloft.

"As witness, and best man by default, it falls to me to offer the toast to the happy couple. This is an old Gaelic toast I believe both the bride and the Captain will appreciate. "May those that love you, love you. And those that don't love you, may God turn their hearts. And if He cannot turn their hearts, may He turn their ankles, so you may know them by their limping."

"Thank you, Joel," Mary said, wiping away tears of laughter.

John said, "Be careful what you ask for, Joel. Soon the whole ship's company may be walking like Igor in those old horror movies."

Mary cut the cake the Captain had provided, and Joel helped pass out slices to everyone. John even opened the door and invited Austin and Dakota in for refreshments, with the Captain's permission. They accepted the cake with relish, but declined the champagne as they were still on duty.

After the wine was gone and the cake and other refreshments fairly well demolished, John stood up. Collecting the glasses and replacing them on the trolley, he opened the door one more time. "Gentlemen, this is your last warning. Unless you want to be thoroughly embarrassed, and shame this good lady as well, I strongly suggest you take your leave. I intend to start our honeymoon in about ten seconds, and I'd just as soon not have an audience."

The men took his words in the good natured spirit in which they were intended, and headed towards the door. Mary walked them out, and as John closed the door behind them, Mary stepped into his arms. "John, you know you really are a silver-tongued devil."

John grinned. "I never thought I spoke all that well."

Mary smiled. "I never said anything about your skills as a speaker, did I?"

Chapter 19

Mary and John were awakened the next morning by the sound of someone pressing the buzzer at the cabin door. Grabbing his pajama bottoms and robe, John gave his new wife a quick kiss and instructions to wait right there for him to return. He closed the bedroom door on his way to answer the buzzer.

Mary could hear two men talking in the next room, but was unable to make out what they were saying. John opened the bedroom door and came in first, and said, "Unless you want to give Austin a show, wife, I suggest you make yourself decent."

No sooner had Mary slipped her robe over her shoulders and pulled the covers up, Austin carried in a tray with what appeared to be a large breakfast. Mary said, "Austin, aren't you with the security staff? Why were you assigned to bring in breakfast? I thought there's be a steward assigned to us."

Austin looked a little sheepish as he carefully placed the loaded tray on the table. "Yes, ma'am, there is a steward. I met him at the door and brought the tray in on my own." He looked as if he wasn't certain what to say next, and spent some time rearranging dishes and silverware. After a long pause, he looked up at John. "You see, sir, I wanted to talk to you, way from Dakota and anyone else in the crew. There are some things going on I don't understand, and I don't really feel comfortable about.

I thought since you were being sent right back as soon as we made the next port, it would be safe to ask you two some questions."

John and Mary exchanged glances. "Austin, why don't you take this lovely breakfast out into the front room, and wait for us," Mary asked. "I want to put on something, then John and I will join you in just a few minutes."

Austin again gathered up the tray, and made his way into that served as the living room. John closed the bedroom door and turned to Mary. "Do you think we dare trust him? I mean, what do you make of this sudden interest in us" just two days ago, he was ready to separate us from our immortal souls, and now he's Mister Nice guy."

"I think he's really sincere, John," Mary said. "He spoke to me when we were on our way here, and he was very cordial, and I don't think his interest is phony. Why don't we just see what he wants, and try to gauge his honesty as we go. But if I get up to leave the room, don't tell him any more. And if you get up to leave, I'll stop as well."

"Alright, Mary. Whatever you say. Since we're married now, I guess you're the boss," John said with a theatrical sigh. It earned him a punch in the shoulder from his "boss."

John and Mary both got dressed quickly and joined Austin in the front room. Sitting down to a breakfast that was much more than they would have received in the dining hall, Mary asked Austin if he would care to join them. When he said he could eat a bite, Mary handed him her bread plate and told him to help himself.

"Austin," John said, "tell me the truth, please. I think we can trust you. Are there any Listeners in this suite at all? Anything we need to be worried about?"

"No sir, Mr. Finestre. This is the VIP Suite. How would it look for someone to monitor conversations between heads of state? That's why I'm glad they put you two here, so I could come talk to you without Dakota."

Mary set her coffee cup down and leaned forward, really interested now. "Why without Dakota, Austin? I thought you and he were partners."

"Yes, ma'am, we are partnered on duty, but that doesn't mean it was my choice. He's got these ideas that seem strange to me. He thinks all our passengers are useless, that because they're old, he says they're breathing up all his air. We need to 'get rid of the dead wood,' he says."

"And you don't feel that way?"

"No, sir! When I was growing up, the most important people in my life were my Granny and Pa. I loved those two old people more than anything in this life. When they died in that awful crash, I thought my life was over. That was why I volunteered for the Elder-Shuttle, to get the chance to interact with people your age again. I didn't expect it to be...you know, like this,"

John and Mary looked at each other, then at Austin. "Austin," Mary said, laying her hand on Austin's arm, "you said you wanted to ask us some questions. What is it you want to know?"

Austin looked from one to the other, as if trying to judge whether or not they could be trusted. "I wanted to know how things got to be the way they are. I feel really foolish, coming to you like this, but since Pa died, there's no one you're age I can talk to. I don't understand the government, how things came about, why don't we have contact with any other countries anymore. I remember when I was little, my mother talked about going to Europe, but now no one goes anywhere, unless it's on the Shuttle. I want to know why."

John poured more coffee for them all and leaned back against the sofa. "Austin, will you be missed for a while I mean, if you're here for more than a few minutes, will you be in trouble?"

"No, sir. I'm off duty as of 0-900 hours. I'm off until 2100. No one will say anything at all about where I spend my time."

"Austin," John asked, "how old are you? You were born, I'm guessing around the turn of the century, weren't you?"

"Yes, sir. I was born on 2001. So I just turned 25 last March."

"Do you remember anything in particular happening around the time you were, oh, say, 6 or so? It would have been around what we used to call Halloween, when the kids used to dress up and go door to door for candy. Do you recall anything in particular?"

"Well, yes sir. I remember that was when my mom and dad both lost their jobs, and we had to move out of our house. It seemed like it was happening to everyone we knew. My family, and my Uncle Bob's family all had to move in with Granny and Pa. I'm not sure why that happened, though. I just remember eating a lot of pasta and casseroles. And Dad had to give his big truck back, and he started taking the bus everywhere."

"What happened in 2007, Austin, was the biggest stock market crash in history. It was even bigger than the one in 1929. I bet your dad was involved in Day Trading in some way, wasn't he." Austin nodded in silent assent. "Almost everyone who had a computer was back then. When the bottom dropped out of all the tech stocks at once, and Microsoft started to flounder, everybody was caught with their pants down. Almost everybody involved lost everything. People had mortgaged their houses to buy stock. It seemed like a good idea at the time, until the investment that had been returning fifty percent began to dip, then became non-existent. Then they had to repay loans with monies they didn't have. Then, to add insult to injury, by that time, anyone who could, drove a big Sports Utility Vehicle, like what I bet your dad had. Those monsters only got around 13 miles to the gallon. Then the price of gas went through the roof, from $1.50 a gallon to $7.00 a gallon. When a man couldn't pay his house payment, he surely couldn't afford to put gas in his truck. And most people bought them on leases, and they couldn't sell them, so they had to stand a repossession. By that time, bankruptcy was a thing of the past, so people lost everything they had. It became a struggle to keep body and soul together. If a person could find a job, even sweeping streets or cleaning out toilets, he took it.

"Then, a man came along with a plan to fix everything. He fixed prices, so no one would be overcharged. He set ceilings on wages, so there wouldn't be such a huge gap between rich and poor. Finally, he gave every man who wanted to work a job within the government or pseudo-government agencies. People were so elated to have food on the table and a stable place to live, they voted a solid ticket to put him in office over and over.

"But then, he drove married women out of the workplace. There was no more birth control, so women had to stay home to tend their children, then child care centers were closed. Citizens were censored in their daily activities, and were even monitored in their own homes. Do you understand what I'm talking about, Austin?"

"When you were living with your grandmother," Mary asked, "did she ever talk about the Second World War, or do you remember watching something called the History Channel on television? Back before your Granny was born, in Germany, a man named Adolph Hitler came to power at the end of a great depression. Because he was able to give the people prosperity and security, they gave him the reins of government. Do you remember hearing anything like that?"

"Yes, ma'am, I think so. Was he that little guy with the funny mustache the Three Stooges used to make fun of?"

"That's him, alright," Mary answered. "But he wasn't a comical character. He was a wicked, evil man. He not only got Germany out of poverty, but he managed to enslave a whole race of people, just because they were different. Hitler segregated groups of people by their country of origin. Then he singled out the ones he didn't like, and sent them to labor camps."

"Mr. And Mrs. Finestre, you're beginning to frighten me. This is all starting to sound too familiar."

"I know, Austin," John said. "And did you know that, above the gates to the camps, there was always a sign that read, 'Work will make you free'?"

Chapter 20

"That's the President's slogan, isn't it, Mr. Finestre? Why should that mean anything special. It seems to me that if you work hard enough, you can get financial freedom. Isn't that what it means?"

Mary leaned over. She tried to describe it as gently as she could. "No, Austin. That's not exactly correct. The camps Hitler used weren't just work camps. They were really death camps. The idea was to get as much work out of the internees as possible, before they dropped dead or were executed. I'm afraid that's what the government has in mind for the passengers on this Shuttle. We are going to the space station to work, until we can't work any more, then we will be kept on life support for the organ donation program. Does that sound like something a caring government would do?"

John joined in. "The reason our country no longer has contact with the outside anymore is for the exact same reason. Other cultures revere their elderly, while our great land tends to see us like your partner Dakota, just something breathing up all their air. And now, it seems, we are seen as spare part repositories,"

Austin rose and paced about the room. He took out his handkerchief and wiped his eyes, and Mary could see they had touched him with the truth.

"Mr. And Mrs. Finestre, I don't know what to say, exactly. I never meant for any thing like this to happen. I just can't imagine something like this going on, especially with our own government. I mean, aren't they supposed to watch out for the citizens' best interest, and all that? Where is our best interest when they condemn a whole generation to a living death. It's not fair. IT'S NOT FAIR!" He slammed his fist down on the desk near the door, and Mary winced at the sound. She was afraid one of the guards outside may have heard it.

"Austin, is anyone outside now?" Mary asked.

Wiping his eyes again, Austin answered, "No, Ma'am. I told him I would look after you two. He wanted a few minutes alone with his girl, anyway, and I told him to take as much time as he needed. They're engaged, and as soon as they marry, she'll have to leave the service, so he's trying to get in as much quality time as he can." He smiled a teary smile.

Walking to Austin, Mary gave him the one thing she knew he really needed at that moment. She held out her arms and gave him a huge hug. She found it hard to keep from crying herself, but she managed to contain the tears for his sake . Holding him close, Mary felt him shudder as he cried in earnest. She found it rare that a man of his stature could actually weep in an old woman's arms; it made her realize just how close he really was to his grandparents. She let him get out of his system, and when she heard him give a loud sniff, she pulled back.

"Are you alright now?"

"Yes, ma'am. Thank you," he said as he wiped his face, somewhat embarrassed.

Mary patted his cheek. "Don't worry. This will never leave the room. I promise you."

John had walked into the bedroom to give Austin a little privacy, and when he heard it was all clear, came back and sat on the sofa. "Can you come back again tomorrow? Do you think you'd be missed, or someone would notice anything out of the ordinary if you spent time here?"

"No, sir. So long as I let Justin have time to see his girl, he'll never breathe a word. And it's my off time, so no one will miss me from duty. I'm new to the ship and to the service, so no one knows for sure what I do with spare time. Did you really want me to come back?"

He was so anxious, he reminded John of a puppy being offered a treat. "Yes, Austin, we really want you to come back.

Every day, if you like. But please be sure to ring the buzzer and don't just walk in. We are still on our honeymoon." John couldn't help but laugh when the big security guard blushed to the tops of his ears.

Mary stood up. "Austin, I think it's wise if you take up your position outside, now. I wouldn't want Justin to come back early and think you were derelict in your duty. Now, we're not trying to throw you out," she said, when she saw his expression fall. "I'm really trying to keep you and us out of trouble. And tomorrow, I want you to score us an extra plate and an extra cup so you can actually join us for breakfast, without having to share utensils."

By his smile, she could see she had just made his whole trip. John stood and shook his hand, and Mary hugged him again. When he pulled out of her arms, Austin looked at John again and said, "Oh, what the hell" and gave him a big bear hug. John grinned a him, and punched him on the shoulder.

"Thanks, Mr. Finestre. I just miss my Pa so much. Sometimes, I just need to be close to someone."

As he walked out the door, John told him in a whisper, "Any time you need another hug, just come on back. If you want, we can't take their place, but we can stand in if you'll let us."

Austin looked over from his post beside the door, gave John a perfect salute and smiled a big, goofy smile.

Chapter 21

John pushed the door shut. When he had secured the lock, he turned and found Mary directly behind him. Putting his arm around her waist, he guided her towards the sofa, and sat with her. He filled the coffee cups, fixed her's and handed her one, already knowing exactly how much cream and sugar she took.

"Ooh, John, you are so good. You know how I take my coffee. You know which side of the bed I prefer. What else have you already figured out?"

"Well, let's see." he said as he nuzzled just below her ear. "I know that no matter how long you've been in bed, your feet are cold. You like cake better than sandwiches, especially if the cake has lots of frosting. You don't like champagne much, and I bet that's because it's not sweet enough." She just nodded, leaning her head more to the side so he could have better access. "I know you've lost interest in that cup of coffee you've been holding."

Mary stood up, drawing John with her. Just as they were about to close the bedroom door, the buzzer sounded. Mary laughed a John's sudden look of fury.

"That's it, Mary. Airman Cloyd is definitely out of the will." John yelled towards the door, "Whoever it is, we don't want any. Go away."

Laughing uproariously, Mary stepped in front of John to cover his "embarrassment" and opened the door. Instead of Austin on guard duty, it was someone she hadn't met. The Captain waited patiently for her to admit him.

"Good morning, Captain Kavanagh," Mary said stepping aside so he could enter. "You have to forgive my new husband. He seems to have this strange idea that we shouldn't be interrupted on our honeymoon"

"I do apologize, Mr. and Mrs. Finestre. I realize this is

an untimely intrusion, but it couldn't be helped. In about thirty six hours, we will be taking your son's shuttle craft aboard, Mrs. Finestre. I just thought you would like a bit of advance notice. Instead of waiting until we arrived at Skylab 6, I was able to contact ground control and avert their flight so we could rendevous ahead of schedule. Of course, if you would like to remain onboard with us for the balance of the trip, that's fine as well. I just took it upon myself to make things easier for all concerned."

By then John had gotten himself in more control, stepped to Mary's side and took her hand. "We both appreciate that, Captain. Is there anything else we need to know?"

"I know this wasn't covered before, but I was just informed myself. Due to the circumstances of your untimely departure, it will be necessary for one of our security staff to accompany you. Not that we expect anything untoward to happen, it's more for your protection, and to make certain that you arrive safely back at the aerodrome."

"Captain," Mary asked, "have you decided yet who will be chosen to accompany us?"

"There's a new security officer with us this trip who's volunteered. I believe you met him last night. Tall, blond, the clean shaven one you spoke with on the way to these quarters, Mrs. Finestre. His name is Austin Fitzhugh. I hope that won't create a problem.'

"No, I don't believe so," John answered. "Was there a specific reason Mr. Fitzhugh volunteered?"

"Apparently there was some difficulty about his leaving home for an extended period as he is the only son, and we've just gotten word that his father passed away. He's been granted compassionate leave. Regardless of the circumstances, I believe it is just as well, as he doesn't fit in well with the rest of the security staff. There seems to be something about him that just rubs the other men wrong."

"John," Mary asked, with a twinkle, "don't you think it might be better if one of the other crew members accompanied us? I told you how intimidated I was that first night in the dining hall. I'd hate to feel that way all the way back home."

John caught on to her ploy immediately. "Yes Captain, I agree. It might really be too stressful for my bride to travel all the way back under those conditions."

The Captain looked perplexed. "I don't know why he would have intimidated you, Mrs. Finestre. He is one of the most gentle men in my crew. As a matter of fact, that's why the other men have a problem with him. Someone started a rumor that Airman Fitzhugh was homosexual. I really don't know if they have cause or not, but I think you can understand I can't allow that kind of dissension aboard my ship."

John let go of Mary's hand. "I think we can handle this, Captain. So long as you instruct Mr. Fitzhugh to limit the use of his weapon to truly threatening situations."

"I don't think that's going to be any problem, Mr. Finestre. Mr. Fitzhugh won't be armed, as this will be a civilian flight. As I'm certain you're aware, no weapons of any kind are allowed in non military flights,"

"I think we can get along just fine, then. It's just that he's so big, then with a side arm he's even more formidable. I just was very frightened of him."

"Mary, dear, if the Captain said everything would be alright, I don't believe we'll have any problems out of Mr. Fitzhugh." John leaned over as if to give her a kiss, and whispered in her ear, "Don't over act."

Mary smiled at him. "Yes, dear," she answered to both questions.

John offered the Captain his hand. "Now, if that's all, Captain Kavanagh, Mrs. Finestre and I would like to pick up where we left off."

The Captain smiled and shook John's hand. As he

turned to leave Mary said, "Oh, and Captain? Would you tell that nice young man outside that we are not to be disturbed for the next...oh, three hours or so."

Captain Kavanagh grinned at John and nodded as he closed the door behind him.

John pulled Mary to him. "You really gave great confidence in me, don't you? I'm not 17 anymore."

Mary stepped out of John's arms and pulled him towards the bedroom. "I know you're not 17 you old fool. I don't want a 17 year old. I want you, and right now. After that, we'll see what you can do with a little extra encouragement."

John followed her willingly. "You, Mrs. Finestre, are truly a silver tongued devil. And you talk pretty good, too."

John managed to kick the bedroom door shut before Mary had his trousers around his ankles.

Chapter 22

Twenty-seven uninterrupted hours later, a very tired pair of newlyweds met the incoming shuttle passengers at the gate to the docking bay. Even though she couldn't keep from grinning like a school girl every time she looked at John, Mary wasn't able to keep the tears of happiness back when not only Jimmy, but her entire family came through the concourse.

"Ma," Jimmy said, as he hugged his mother tightly, "everything's going to be alright now. There's no need for you to cry." He acted truly worried about her. Mary wondered if anything had happened she needed to be really worried about, aside from her own government trying to harvest her spare parts.

Wiping tears from her face, Mary kissed his cheek. "I'm not upset, Jimmy. I'm just overjoyed that I've got my entire family here. Is there something I need to worry about?"

The Captain stepped forward and offered his hand to Jimmy. "Mr. Callahan, I'm Captain Marc Kavanagh. I'd like to welcome you and your family aboard my vessel. While we're re-supplying your ship, why don't you take your family to Mr. and Mrs. Finestre's suite and make yourselves comfortable? We shouldn't be more than three hours."

Jimmy agreed, and rounded up the entire group. As John led the way, Jimmy pulled his mother back. "Ma," Jimmy whispered, "did I hear the Captain correctly? Did he say 'Mr. and Mrs. Finestre?' It seems there's a lot going on that needs explaining. From both of us."

When they reached the VIP suite, everyone crowded inside. John said to Jimmy, "Mr. Callahan, when you and I first met, you wore NASA uniforms, but now you're in a civilian flight suit. Is something going on we need to know about, aside from the obvious?"

Jimmy sank wearily into the nearest chair. "When I saw

you and Ma at the Aerodrome I was shocked. Fiona never told me she had gotten Ma a ticket."

"Jimmy, why were you worried? I thought you believed in the Elder Shuttle program?"

"I did, Ma. At least in theory. Then I found out what was going on at Skylab 6. I mean, really going on. Not just voluntary work, if a person chose, but forced labor, and organ harvesting. No one should have to agree to that, regardless of their age. I mean, it's illegal to use animals for transplant or research anymore but it seems as if the government has relegated anyone past retirement age to a status below animals."

"John," Mary said. "Before we go any further, I believe some introductions are in order. You already know my son, Jimmy. The lady seated on the arm of his chair is his wife, Johnica. In the other chair is my daughter Erin, and her husband Neal is that good looking guy standing behind her. Erin's children are lined up on the sofa, in order there's Sean, William, Meghan and the one on the end who started this whole mess, Fiona. On the floor in front of them are Jimmy's two, Robert and Jamison." Mary turned to her family as she took John's hand. "Now, everyone, even though the Captain spoiled my surprise, I'd like to introduce you all to my new husband, Gianni Finestre. I call him John. I don't think he'd object to yo all doing the same."

"I know this came as a shock to all of you," John said, as he put his arm around Mary. "It sort of did to me, too. But when you reach our age, it's best not to waste time."

Erin rose and went to embrace her mother. "Ma, I'm glad you've found someone to make you happy. I would have liked a little warning, though. I mean, two days, come on! Isn't that a little sudden, even for you?"

When her family was through laughing, Mary explained to a bewildered John, "When their father and I met, we dated for an entire month before we got married and Jimmy was born

8 months after our wedding day."

John noticed the red creeping up from Jimmy's shirt collar. "Mr. Callahan, I think I can assure you that your mother and I will not present you with a baby brother or sister any time soon. That said, can we at least have your blessing?"

Johnica was the first to go to John and offer a hug. The rest of the family followed in quick succession. "Sean," Mary said when everyone had resumed their seats, "I think its time you tell us what you know about this."

"Uncle Jimmy came to the house one night and he was furious. When he got Fiona aside and started to yell and scream at her about killing her own grandmother, I had to step in.."

"What do you mean, 'killing her own grandmother?' Jimmy, tell me what's going on."

"As I said, Ma," Jimmy said, "when I saw you at the Aerodrome, I was shocked, to say the least. Rumors had been spreading about the real reason behind Skylab 6, and we had just receive official confirmation that morning. I was prepared to resign my commission that Friday anyway, as I refuse to be involved in such a travesty. When I saw you there, I knew I had to do something. And I knew, after seeing you and John together, you wouldn't leave easily without him, so Sean and I conspired to get you out."

"That's right, Granny," Sean took over. When I found out what Uncle Jimmy was carrying on about, we sat down together and worked out a scheme to get you home safely. Uncle Jimmy gave me the codes to the genealogical files in Wilkes Barre, and I hacked into their records and made a few 'corrections.' It's been a long time since I did anything like that. It was a rush. But I still don't understand exactly what's going on."

Fiona told her grandmother, "I thought I saw some of your things come through my line the day you left, Granny, but I wasn't sure. At least, until I picked up the little ceramic figurine and saw the sticker on the bottom that said, 'Robert, Christmas, 2019.' Then I really knew something was terribly wrong. When Uncle Jimmy came to the house, he didn't really yell and scream, but it wouldn't have taken much to convince me anyway. When I saw that porcelain bird, I knew unless we did something, you weren't coming back."

"Jimmy," John asked, "how much time do we have before we have to board?"

Jimmy looked at his watch. "At least two more hours. Why?"

"Mary," John said, "lets take these people into the other room and show them my computer."

"Are you sure, John? Is there enough time? I don't want to be caught with that just when things are looking up."

"That's why we're going in the other room." Opening the door, he said, "I know this is not the best venue for watching what you're about to see, but I'm afraid you'll all have to perch on the bed and floor for the next 45 minutes or so. I think this will be very enlightening.

Bewildered, the family followed John into the largest of the two bedrooms, while Mary went to the second bedroom to collect the extra pillows and blankets. When everyone had made themselves as comfortable as possible, John retrieved his "Apple" from the closet. "Ladies and Gentlemen, you are about to see something which has been banned in our great land for many years, both in technology and content. I hope you are all both amazed and disgusted with what you are about to see."

Connecting the power cord to the nearest outlet, John inserted a video tape, dimmed the lights, and sat at the head of the bed, next to his wife. Pushing the button on the remote, he said, "Most of you are too young to remember, but this was recorded from a program on the History Channel, before it was forced off the air for telling the truth about world history. I understand the network still broadcasts in Britain, but not in the

U.S. The program is about something that happened before any of us were born, but happened in my parents' lifetime. What you are about to see is some old newsreel footage on the Holocaust."

Sean looked back at John. "John. what is the Holocaust? I mean, I know what the word means, but what does it have to do with us, now?"

"Before I answer your questions, Sean, I want you to watch the program. Some of the things in it may anger you, or make you cry or even make you sick, but it's important that you see every foot of film in this cassette. After you've seen it, I'll answer any questions any of you may have."

The family watched scenes of the liberation of Auschwitz, the conditions at Ravensbruk and the mass graves at Treblinka ran across the screen. Images of men being shot in the back of the head, positioned so they would fall forward into the grave they had just dug, vied with footage of Hitler and Eve Braun at their retreat in the Alps. The dismal image Warsaw Ghetto was in contrast to scenes of Nazi wedding celebrations and the Jungenkorps gatherings. Photographs of the plenty following the Great Depression played against the deprivation of the Jews, homosexuals and dissidents of the 1930's in the Third Reich.

Erin passed out tissues to every one as they watched, and Mary noticed there wasn't a dry eye in the room by the time the film was finished. Twelve year old Robert buried his face in his father's lap, so no one would see him cry. John stopped the tape as the final credits came on. "I think everyone has seen enough for now. I have a whole collection of World War II news reel footage that I recorded from the History Channel and Turner Networks before they were forced to shut down and the original footage destroyed. Something told me to bring these tapes onboard with me for the trip. I was fortunate enough to be assigned to a really dumb customs agent who thought this was an old PC and the cassettes were software. On the way back, if you're up to it, you can watch more footage."

John very carefully removed the tape and returned it to it's carrying case, then placed the TV-VCR back in the closet, where it would be safe from prying eyes. "Mary," John said when he was done, "would you mind calling down and having some sandwiches or something sent up. I don't know about any one else, but I could really go for something a little more substantial than what we've had the last day or so."

Mary shoved John a hard enough to propel him off the edge of the bed where he had just perched. "And whose fault was that, Mr. Finestre? Every time I tried to.... Well, anyway, I'll see what I can have sent up in a hurry."

Erin and Johnica exchanged looks and went with Mary into the sitting room.

Chapter 23

After Mary had called down for some refreshments, she sat with Erin and Johnica on the sofa' after a few minutes of small talk about the family's flight, Erin couldn't hold back any longer. "Alright, Ma, give. How did you come to be married to that good looking guy just a few days into the trip? And how much trouble are you really in?"

"John and I got married the second full day out of the Aerodrome. Even though we just met, I feel as if I've known him for years. He makes me laugh. He's strong enough to let me make a decision concerning me, without trying to convince me to do it his way." Mary leaned forward, and said in a conspiratorial tone, "And best of all, every thing works very well, regardless of our ages."

Erin laughed with abandon at her mother's off color jest, but Johnica looked rather nonplused. "Come now Mother Callahan, you don't mean to imply that you and Mr. Finestre have consummated your marriage. That's absurd, at your age."

Erin groaned out loud. Mary said to Johnica, "Yes, that's exactly what I'm implying. When I said everything worked very well, I wasn't speaking of his ability to fix machinery. Everything works, without any chemical stimulation, and I'm extremely happy. Just wait until Jimmy's our age, and see if his libido has faltered. I can ell you right now, his father's never did, right up until the day he died."

Johnica studied her shoes, while Erin tried very hard not to laugh out loud at her mother's speech. After a few minutes of watching Johnica watch her shoes, Erin leaned over and touched her knee. "Johnica, honey, is everything al right between you and Jimmy? He's my brother, and if something was wrong, I'd like to know, too."

Johnica continued to stare at the floor. Erin noticed tears beginning to flow. "I don't know why, but since Jimmy started on the Shuttle project last year, he's just not been interested in anything like that. I don't know why, but I'm afraid it might be me. And since this has been going on, I'm afraid I've been nasty to him as well, just really short tempered about everything. I don't want him to leave me." Johnica broke down and began to sob in earnest.

Mary put her arm around her daughter-in-law. "Johnica, to begin with, your husband has a very high-pressure job. I think you can rest assured he's not playing hide the sausage with anyone else. Perhaps he's been worried about his job. But to tell you the honest-to-god truth, I don't think he was really happy with his assignment. You heard him in the bedroom, how he'd found out what was really going on. I don't blame him for not having any desire for anything but a remedy to this mess,"

"Maybe you're right, Mother Callahan."

Mary hugged her, hard, then. "First off, Johnica, let's drop that 'Mother Callahan'' crap. I feel as if I were in some old sitcom on television. Please, PLEASE call me 'Ma' or at least 'Mary.' It's still my name, you know."

Johnica gave her a watery smile, dried her eyes, stood and moved towards the bedroom door. "Okay, then, Ma. How many bedrooms does this suite have?"

Mary and Erin smiled at her. 'There's two bedrooms, dear, each with it's own private bath. Why?"

"Would you and John mind terribly if I used one of those rooms to have a private talk with my husband? A VERY private talk, for about forty-five minutes or so?"

"Not at all, dear. Tell you what; you go in through that door to your right, and I'll go get Jimmy. If you're not out by the time your ship is ready to take off, I'll send Robert and Jamison in after you. That should give you some incentive to mind the time. Oh, and by the way, in case you hadn't figured it out yet, this is the VIP suite. There are no Listeners

ANYWHERE. I guess that kind of gives you an extra incentive."

Johnica hugged Mary one last time, before she went into the bedroom. Mary went to the other room and called her son. "Jimmy, can I see you for a minute, please."

"Sure, Ma. Is everything alright?"

"Jimmy," said Erin, "may I have your wrist watch for a little while, please?"

"What on earth do you want my watch for?"

Mary was grinning at him like a cat who had been into the cream. "Just give your sister your watch. That's right. Now then, I want you to go through that door on the right, and I bet you'll have a surprise waiting for you."

Jimmy looked between his mother and sister, becoming more bewildered by the second. "Okay, Ma. Whatever you say," he said.

Jimmy walked to the bedroom door, opened it, and saw his wife lying naked across the covers. Peering around the door at his mother, he asked with a grin, "Ma, do you and Erin think you can keep the boys occupied for, oh, about a half-hour or so?"

Erin and Mary were walking towards the other bedroom. "I think so, big brother. But you know, you two will miss the eats Ma called out for."

As Jimmy shut the door, Erin heard him say, "No, sis, I think we'll have plenty to eat."

Mary and her daughter laughed as they went to join the rest of the family. John asked, "What's up?" and both women lost control, falling into gales of laughter.

Revelation dawned on the men when Jamison asked, "Granny, are Mom and Dad coming back to eat with us?"

John answered for her, with a sly glance to his wife, "No, son, I think you're Mom and Dad had some things they wanted to discuss before we take off."

Neal reached out to his wife. John saw the way his mind was working and said, "And before you ask, Neal, there are no more places for you and Erin to have a discussion right now. So get those thoughts out of your mind."

Erin's kids and all the adults shared the joke, while the two younger boys just shrugged, as if to say, "Adults, go figure."

The food arrived, and Mary and Erin pushed the trolley into the bedroom. "Wouldn't we be more comfortable in the sitting room?" John asked.

Mary laughed. "No, John, I think we would be distinctly uncomfortable. It seems my daughter-in-law and your stepson are very...shall we say... vociferous? I really would prefer not to have to listen to sound effects with my meal."

Chapter 14

When Jimmy rejoined the company, they had finally made their way into the front room. He eased into a chair vacated by his nephew, Sean. "Before anyone asks," Jimmy announced, "Johnica's in the shower right now, and should be out in just a minute. And yes, everything is just fine." This last word was said with very self-satisfied smile.

Mary looked at her daughter. "No, Erin, there's no time for you and Neal to have a discussion of your own right now."

"Ma, you have the filthiest mind of any old lady I know," Erin said with a laugh.

"Why do you think I married her?" asked John.

"I'm crushed," Mary responded. There I thought it was for my girlish figure or perhaps my sparkling wit."

"Well, those did enter into the equation. But it was your mind that first attracted me."

Jimmy laughed along with the rest of the adults. "See, Sis. I told you some men are really attracted to women for their minds. It's not all physical."

Johnica came into the room in time to hear what her husband said. "I heard that, James Callahan. Alright, if you're so attracted to women's minds, there's that girl that works at the market on the corner back home. Do you know the one I mean?"

"I think so," Jimmy answered as Johnica sat on the arm of his chair and he put his arm around her hips. "Do you mean the one with the large...ah...assets?" he said, gesturing a very large bosom with his hand.

Neal and John laughed. Johnica said, "Yes, that's the one. Did you know she's in college during the day, and she's working towards her doctorate in bio-engineering?"

"No, I didn't know that. I'm sorry, I never really talked to her." Jimmy was a little embarrassed at this.

"Alright then, Mr. Visual Perception. At least can you tell me what color her eyes are?"

Jimmy thought for a few minutes. Neal stepped in for him. "Joni, think I know the girl you're talking about. But I don't think any man alive has even noticed if she HAD eyes, let alone what color they are."

Everyone in the room laughed as Erin coshed her husband over the head with the throw pillow she had been leaning against. When the buzzer at the door sounded, John motioned for them to carry on, as he went to open the door.

"Austin," John said, "come in and meet Mary's family."

Austin came in warily, as if he didn't quite know what to expect. Carrying his duffle in one hand, he carefully placed it on the floor as Mary went through the litany of names of the others in the room. "And everybody, this is Austin. He's the Security Officer assigned to travel with us back home. He's a very nice young man, and he's planning to remain with his family once he's back home."

"Mr. And Mrs. Finestre, the Captain asked me to fetch you all to the departure area. Our ship is ready to take off. Do you have everything packed and ready to go?"

"Yes, I think everything's ready. Fiona," Mary said, "would you mind checking the closets and drawers one more time to make certain I got everything?"

"Sure, Granny. Is there anything in particular I should look for?"

"No," Mary answered, "not that I can think of. Just make certain you check the closets in both bedrooms and the cabinets in the baths, too."

Fiona left to check for anything that may have been forgotten, while Austin helped Neal and Jimmy gather up the few things John and Mary had brought on board with them. The "Apple" was securely packed in Mary's case for concealment. When Austin began to pick up that one bag, Jimmy stepped forward and grabbed it first. "I better get this one, son," Jimmy said. "If my Ma's perfume gets broken, there'll be hell to pay. You know how women can be."

"Oh, I understand, Mr. Callahan. My Mom and Grandma were the same way. Only certain people were allowed to handle their things. How about if I take the satchels, then? Are there any breakables in here, Mrs. Finestre?"

"No, Austin, go ahead and take those. Are you sure you can handle two of our bags and your duffle bag, too? You know, John and I can carry something. For that matter, we can all take one thing, and still have at least a half a dozen hands left over."

Jimmy stepped to the door. "We've got everything now, Ma. So if you can round up Fiona, we can get going. I for one am anxious to be on my way."

"John," Mary asked, "will you get Fiona, please. Make sure she's got everything, though. I'd hate to get halfway home and realize I'd left my curling iron or something."

"Yes, dear. I'll get Fiona. You just concentrate on herding this lot towards the docking bay."

John met Fiona as she was coming out of the second bedroom, where her uncle had recently entertained her aunt so well. "Did you find anything we left behind?"

Fiona laughed, then blushed when it registered who she was talking to. "Well, I did find something. But I don't think it's your's or Granny's. I think Aunt Joni let something behind."

John looked at Fiona intensely. "Fiona, is everything alright? Mary, come here a minute please. I was just talking to Fiona, and she went all red. You don't think anything's wrong, do you?"

Mary went to her husband. "Fiona, what's wrong?"

Fiona was unable to control herself, and sat down on the couch laughing. She reached into her jacket pocket and took out a small wad of fabric. "I think Aunt Joni left these behind after she and Uncle Jimmy had their talk."

John held out his hand. Fiona looked at her grandmother. At Mary's nod, Fiona handed the scrap of fabric to him. John turned his back to everyone else in the room, and held up, for his and Mary's eyes only, a pair of tiny silk panties. Mary hid her face in her husband's chest.

"Jimmy," John called, "could we see you for a minute?" John folded up the panties and held them hidden in his hand.

"What's wrong John?"

"You might want to wait a few seconds to let your wife finish dressing," John said as he pressed the drawers into Jimmy's hand. "I don't want her to catch cold."

Jimmy leaned over to John and whispered something in his ear. When John laughed, Mary looked up at him and asked what was so all fired funny now.

"Jimmy just asked me if Fiona found his boxers. It appears he's misplaced those as well."

"John," Mary laughed, "when we leave this ship, do you realize the reputation you are going to have with the housekeeping staff? Two beds messed up, and underwear scattered hither and yon."

"Don't worry about it, my dear. The other women will just be jealous."

Chapter 25

When the entire party had assembled near Jimmy's shuttle Mary could help but marvel at the size. "Jimmy, is it safe for us to travel in something so small? I mean, there's so many of us and it just seems as if it would be cramped. And I worry about the flight crew. Will there be room for them, too."

"Ma," Jimmy said, as he opened the shuttle door, "you're looking at the flight crew. Neal and I flew this beast here. And don't worry, there's plenty of room. Remember the big Winnebago camper Da's parents used to spend every summer in? This is on the same principle. There's multi-use spaces, and so long as we're not traveling with small children, we'll be just fine."

John poked his head inside the shuttle door. "Multi-use spaces. Does that mean what I think it does? The kitchen table folds back to make a bed, that sort of thing?"

"That's it, John. The only real draw back , aside from the lack of privacy, is the lack of bathroom facilities."

"Whoa, hold it right there, Mr. Callahan," Austin finally spoke up. "Lack of bathroom facilities? I really don't see any way to carry a Porta Potty with us. And I for one am not going outside."

"No, Austin." Jimmy laughed as he clapped Austin on the shoulder. "What I meant was there's only one bathroom, and only a shower, no full tub. We just have to limit our individual time in the necessary, so everyone will have equal time."

When everyone had crowded inside the shuttle, Neal and Jimmy were busily collapsing tables against walls and lifting up seats. There were modified flight seats, with head rests and seatbelts, which appeared to have conversion features. Enough were set up for everyone, and Erin made sure all the children were properly seated, including her own grown kids, who she still fussed over as if they were five. Erin and Johnica took their seats directly behind their husbands, who were in the pilot and co-pilot seats, John and Mary behind them. Mary noticed that Austin made it a point to sit all the way in the back, next to Fiona.

Finally, after what seemed like endless preflight checks, they were finally ready to go. The airlock was in place the chock blocks removed, and the little shuttle lifted and hovered briefly as it turned towards the outer bay doors then swept out into space.

When the ship was set on its course towards Earth, Jimmy set the auto-pilot and he and Neal went to join the others. Jimmy showed everyone how to convert the seats from take-off benches to cruise seats, by pulling up the padded arm covers and adjusting the back to a more comfortable position. He finally pulled a bench out from one of the bulkheads to sit on. After Neal had joined him, Mary finally asked what had been troubling her since she and john had received word they were being transported heme.

"Jimmy, where exactly are we going? Neither John nor I have a place to stay, and we won't be separated in the Institution. And we damn sure won't take their cyanide cocktail. So, what do you all propose we do with ourselves?"

"We've all given this a lot of thought, Ma, " Jimmy answered. "We just haven't come up with an answer that will work. And not only do you and John not have a place to go, but none of us do, either. One of the things we were forced to give up, along with our positions, were our houses. The government can't have those of 'impure heritage' in prime housing, after all. So, I guess unless we can come up with something better, we'll have to stake out a bridge to live under."

Sean spoke up. "Uncle Jimmy, what would happen if we just didn't go home?"

Jimmy looked puzzled. "What do you mean, not go

home? We can't just toodle around space for the next hundred years,"

"I know that," Sean said, slightly hurt to be talked to as if he were 10, and hadn't been the one to figure out how to save his grandmother to begin with. "I mean, what would happen if we landed somewhere else, say, Europe? Could we do that?"

Jimmy and Neal looked at each other in surprise. "Well, IF we could get there without crossing U.S. airspace, and IF we can get landing permission from the EU country in question, I suppose it could be done. What do you have in mind, exactly?"

"According to what I saw on John's History Channel tapes, there was something regarding the schedule for the EU's legislative meetings, and how they are held in a different member nation's capital every year. So far as I can figure out, just going by the year and the number of countries in the Union, this year should be London''s turn. Do you think you could put this thing down at Heathrow?"

"Why London, Sean?" John asked. He was beginning to see the method to Sean's madness, but had to make sure they were of a like mind.

"As I said, I figure this year is London's turn to host the meeting of the Nations. There's no one else we can complain to about conditions in the U.S., since the United Nations was thrown out of New York, and disbanded. Why can't we plead our case before the EU? After all, we're all of European extraction. That should give us some rights."

"Even if we can't address the counsel, at least we can have a place to stay that's not under a bridge," Mary said.

"Ma," Neal said gently, "we may still wind up under that bridge. The government confiscated all our combined funds and accounts of any kind. They said we couldn't be enriched through fraudulent means. The only money we have available is the money you make from the sale of your house after Da passed away. And you know that won't last long. Not with all of us to feed and keep."

"Then," Fiona spoke up from the rear of the cabin, "there's Austin. we can't very well expect him to go along with this. I mean, it would cost him his career."

"Mr. And Mrs. Finestre," Austin said as he stood by Fiona's seat, "I would be honored if you would consider me part of your family, and would include me in your travel plans. And I have some funds of my own, at least enough to find a place that will put us up for a while."

"Austin," Fiona said with surprise, "that's so generous."

"Well, since I lost my own grandparents, the short time I've known your grandmother and her husband, they've become almost as important to me as my own were."

Fiona smiled up at Austin, and he was lost.

Chapter 26

Alternating shifts, Neal and Jimmy managed to avoid the American airspace, and set their course for the United Kingdom. As they re-entered Earth's atmosphere, the entire party had returned to their original places, and were securely buckled into their seat harnesses. Coming over the North Sea, headed towards the Irish Sea, Jimmy attempted to contact with London Air Traffic Control.

"Heathrow Tower, this is Commander James Xavier Callahan, late of the United States NASA program. I have under my command a private shuttle craft, identification number Paul-seven-niner zero. I am requesting permission to land my craft at your facility, and I am requesting political asylum for eleven adults and two juveniles."

"Paul-seven-niner-zero, please confirm your country of origin."

'Heathrow Tower, our flight originated in the United States; we rendezvoused with the Elder-Shuttle three days out of port, and picked up two of our party. They are the reason we beg asylum."

"Paul-seven-niner-zero, please set your course for terminal three. We will have representatives of the home Office awaiting your arrival."

"Thank you, Heathrow Tower. ETA is in approximately 17 minutes. Paul-seven-niner-zero, out."

Behind Jimmy, he could hear the kids giving each other high-fives, and heard his sister, Erin, weeping quietly. "Neal," Jimmy said, "I think your wife needs you right now more them I do. Why don't you go on back to her and have Sean come up here. He can handle the controls almost as well as you, anyway."

Neal patted Jimmy on the shoulder as a small, silent thanks, and went back to change places with his son. Sean was overjoyed to have a turn as co-pilot. He flopped into the chair like a small, eager puppy looking for a new treat. "What do I do, Uncle Jimmy? Do you really need me to help fly the ship?"

"Not right now, son. I just thought your dad needed to sit with your mom for now. But as we come close to the landing approach, I'll need you to mind the instruments while I watch the ground. Think you can do that?"

"Isn't this pretty much like the simulator you had me on at NASA a few weeks ago?"

"Yes, it 's exactly like the simulator. Now do you understand why I was so insistent you and your father both came with me to practice? I've been planning something like this for a while. I just didn't anticipate pulling your grandmother's butt out of a sling, which necessitated moving things along rather precipitously."

The runways of Heathrow came into sight. Jimmy called back to make certain everyone was secured in their seats. He contacted the tower again to reaffirm his handing location. As his craft settled down over Terminal Three's runway, Jimmy cut the aft jets, released the hover jets, and gently guided the ship to the ground. With the final bump as the wheels made contact with the ground, Jimmy looked to his tight, and saw his nephew beam at him, as if Sean had just had a personal epiphany. "Well, Sean," Jimmy said as he unfastened his harness and stood to stretch his shoulders, "you've landed your first shuttle. What'd you think?"

Sean stood shakily, and whispered to his uncle, "I think I may have just cum in my pants."

Jimmy laughed and handed Sean his jacket. "I know the feeling, son. Happened to me the first time I landed one of these monsters. You're dad never took to flying. He's a fine passenger, but in the cockpit, he's scared shitless. Just put on the jacket as if you're cold, and no one will know the difference, except maybe another pilot. And they'll understand."

"Uncle Jimmy, does England have a military academy? If it meant I could fly one of these, I'd like to join."

"There used to be one. I think it's called Sandringham, but I don't know if it's still operational. Anyway, I think that was more for the offspring of royalty. If it can be done, though, I think we can work something out. But I thought you wanted to make your living with computers. Has that changed?"

"Well, you see, I figure these are just big computers with wings. So I'll sort of be able to work with computers, and still get to fly."

Neal and John had secured the passenger seats into the non-flight positions, and had the hatch on the airlock ready to open. When the external buzzer sounded, signaling the all-clear, Neal swung the heavy door back and tethered it to the bulkhead. A modified jetway was swung into place from the terminal, and Neal and Jimmy attached the accordion-folded extension to the hatchway. Jimmy retrieved his flight cap from the compartment near the hatch, pulled Sean to his side as his co-pilot, and assembled the rest of the family behind them, with Mary and John in the rear.

Stepping into the jetway, they were first met by an Heathrow security officer, who greeted Jimmy and Sean with a smart salute, and directed them to the main concourse. Ascending into the terminal, Johnica kept the younger children together while Erin held tighter onto Neal's arm. Mary reached for John as she saw Austin take Fiona's hand. John leaned down to Mary, "Well I see something else good did come of this mess after all."

Mary just smiled up at him and caressed the side of his cheek with her free hand. He leaned over to give her a quick kiss. "I just want you to know this is not exactly how I expected to spend our honeymoon, in close quarters with eleven other people."

"I know, darling. But I fully expect you to make it up to me at your earliest convenience."

When they reached the lounge area, they were surprised to see the committee that awaited them. Not only were there a full contingent of security officers, which was to be expected, but what appeared to be a group of dignitaries as well, including a tall, thin middle-aged man in a full-dress military uniform. The senior officer of the security staff stepped forward to greet them. "Commander Callahan, I presume? I'm Major Williams of Heathrow Security. I must say, I don't believe we've had such a stir here since that Nazi landed in Scotland in 1941. I'm pleased you landed safely, and I'd like to welcome your party to our fair city."

Shocked by this greeting, when he had been half expecting immediate incarceration, Jimmy offered his hand to Major Williams. "Major Williams," Jimmy said, "may I introduce my family?

"First, this young gentleman is my co-pilot and nephew, Sean Mulroney, without whom I wouldn't have been able to land with such precision. Next, you see my sons, Robert and Jamison, my nephew William and niece Meghan, followed by my lovely wife, Johnica. My sister Erin and her husband Neal Mulroney, my niece Fiona. Next to Fiona is the young security officer from the Elder-Shuttle, Austin Fitzhugh, who volunteered to accompany us home. Finally, the people who started this, my mother and step father, Mary and John Finestre."

Major Williams greeted each person with a nod and a smile, and began introductions of his own. Jimmy was shocked by the titles thrown about. Finally, he came to the last two, "...and this is Lady Alistair, Duchess of Kent. According to protocol, I should have made introductions in the reverse order, but was asked to do otherwise, as we were afraid we might intimidate you. Finally, I would very much like to make known to you Prince Harry, Duke of Argyle, Commander and Chief of the Royal Air Corps and Chief Secretary of the Home Office."

Nonplused by the last introduction, Jimmy snapped a rigid salute. Mary fell into a deep curtsy, and hissed to her daughter and daughter in-law to follow suit. Finally catching on, the men bowed slightly, still confused. Taking the initiative, and feeling better as time went on, and no one brandished weapons in their direction, Mary elbowed her way to the front. Curtseying deeply again, she said, "Your Grace, it is an honor to meet you." When he gestured for her to rise, she asked, "To what do we owe the honor of your visit, Sir? We had no reason to expect that the fourth in line to the crown would be here to greet us."

"This is more along the lines of official business, madam. There are some things I need to discuss with your party."

"Your Grace," Mary asked, "would it be possible for us to be assigned quarters first, so we may rest and change into something a bit more suitable for a royal audience than these flight suits? You see, Sir, we've been three days in very close quarters, and I think we could all use a little time away from each other."

"I understand completely, my dear. Major Williams, please see that these good people are assigned suitable quarters, not military facilities, but a decent hotel if you please. And see to it that they are first taken round to Oxford High Street. I believe the ladies would like a visit to Marks and Spencers, unless they'd prefer Harrod's. And see to it that everything is put on the household account."

Mary was flabbergasted. "No, Your Grace. Marks and Spencers will do quite nicely. And thank you , Sir, very much." Mary curtseyed again as the Duke turned to leave.

When only the refugees and Major Williams were left, Jimmy said, "Major, what exactly is going on? I thought sure we were going to be confined at least until our story checked out. But I never expected to be put up in a hotel and given *carte blanche* in a department store."

"Come with me, for now, please. I can explain it as we go. First, is there any objection if we take the Underground into the city? It's much faster than traveling on surface streets, and we'll have the security of a private car, as this is the beginning of the line."

John finally found his voice. "I believe I speak for everyone, Major. The quicker we get away from this shuttle and put it behind us, the happier we'll be."

"Good, good," Major Williams said. "I'll have your personal possessions transferred to your hotel. I understand you've been in close quarters for a while, so I've taken the liberty of arranging for you to have an entire floor of a very nice hotel near Hyde Park. If that doesn't meet with your approval, I can make other arrangements, but I thought it best if we kept you close to Parliament. And by reserving the whole floor, it makes security a bit simpler."

"I don't think we'll want to escape, Major," Jimmy said.

"Oh, I wasn't worried about you. I just feel better if we can keep an eye on the comings and goings of, shall we say, others of dubious alliances."

Chapter 27

The younger members of the family were intrigued by the "Tube," having never seen anything like it at home. The adults were still stunned by the attention paid to them by government officials . As it was a Sunday and late in the morning, there was very little pedestrian traffic in the Heathrow Underground station at Terminal Three. The party had moved down the long, circuitous tunnel to the station, then waited only a minute or two for the next train. Sean asked Major Williams, "Major, does the subway run all the time like this?"

Major Williams answered indulgently, "Yes, Mr. Mullroney, at this stop, about every seven minutes or so. Of course, it varies at different stations and lines. This one will take us directly to Oxford High Street, then we'll have government transport fetch us to take us to the hotel. I really didn't expect you to wrestle with parcels on your own."

About twenty minutes after the train left Heathrow, they arrived at the Highgate Station. Mary asked the Major about the lack of pedestrian traffic, and was assured this was usual for a Sunday, as the shops weren't open, with the exception of pharmacies, or as the Major called them, "chemist's shops." Mary wondered how they would shop if the stores wouldn't be open.

When they had walked the two long blocks from the Tube stop to Marks and Spencers, they were greeted by a nattily dressed floor walker, who was waiting outside the front door for them. They were escorted inside, where each member of the group was assigned a sales person of their own , and told to pick out whatever they desired. Seeing the avaricious looks on her grandchildren's faces, Mary told them sternly, "Only get the necessities, please. Remember, we are guests here, and don't wish to seem greedy."

"Mrs. Finestre, I'm certain if we allow the sales staff to

guide their purchases, they will do just fine. After all, you will be here for some time, and you are, after all, guests of His Grace." Major Williams issued instructions to the floor walker, who in turn gave direction to the sales staff. When everyone was finally settled down to their own shopping expedition, Mary found herself with Erin, Johnica and Fiona. Meghan had gone with Robert and Jamison to make sure they behaved themselves.

A middle aged sales woman approached them and spoke to Mary, "Madam, where would you like to begin?"

Mary looked at the woman's name tag. "Well, Mrs. George, I don't really know what we'll need. I thought we'd leave it up to you what departments we need to visit, then we can make our individual choices."

"An excellent decision, Madam. Now, if you all will follow me, we'll go first to Ladies' Formal Wear, then we'll work our way down to the Hall of Food, if that meets with your approval, Madam."

"Yes, certainly, Mrs. George." They followed her to an elevator reserved for the staff, and went to one of the upper floor. There, the women were astounded by the array of finery laid out before them. Mary couldn't help herself. "Mrs. George, why do we need formal gowns? After all, I really don't think we'll be attending any balls while we're here."

"Madam jests," Mrs. George laughed lightly. "Why, for the royal audience, of course. And something else for the gathering of the joint Houses of Parliament."

The four women stopped dead in their tracks as the sales clerks continued on ahead of them. Still not knowing exactly what to make of anything, Mary told them, "I guess we just go along with her for now. At least we'll be the best dressed prisoners in the Tower of London."

When they caught up with the staff, they were taken back yet again by the sheer sumptuousness about them. Fiona had never even seen anything to rival this, and the rest of the women of the family were struck dumb with waves of nostalgia.

Mary was drawn to an outfit with a pair of pale green silk trousers and a floor-length tunic printed with abstract designs in various shades of green and mauve. "Mrs. George, this is quite lovely; I've not seen anything like it in years. Surely this would not be suitable for a royal audience, would it?"

"Why of course it would, Madam. Surely you're familiar with our new Prime Minister, Ms. Narwahli? A lovely young woman with such an adorable baby. She wears just this type of ensemble to all State functions. It's quite the rage, now."

"Mrs. George," Fiona asked, "did I hear you correctly? Your new Prime Minister not only wears slacks in public, but she's a single woman of Indian extraction, with a baby?"

"Why, yes, dear. Is that a problem?"

Mary stepped in to try to explain. "You see, Mrs. George, the United States seems to have become quite xenophobic. Not only aren't people of certain ethnic backgrounds prohibited from holding certain positions within the government, but women are kept out of government all together now. Women with children are forbidden to work outside the home, and unless it is required for one's job, we're forbidden to wear slacks. Recently, it has become illegal for any female who is unmarried to have her hair cut, as if it adds to our subservience to males."

Mrs. George and the rest of her staff were astounded. "Madam, allow me to welcome you to the free world. This is London, one of the world's oldest and most modern cities. As a matter of fact, Madam, if I may be so bold, after we have selected your outfits, may I suggest we send the gentlemen on to the hotel, and I will call in our salon staff in order that you ladies may enjoy whatever services you desire."

Fiona looked at her grandmother. "Granny, do you think Austin would like me with short hair? And how about a little color, you know, to bring out the red more? My hair's just so stringy since I can't have it cut any more. What do you think?"

Mary hugged her. Mrs. George said, "Miss, I think he'll like you if your head was shaved. But if you want it cut, highlighted, whatever, it's your hair, and it's up to you. Don't ever worry about what some man will think of your hair. If he's in the relationship for the hair, give him a sack full of it and tell him to bugger off. And we have a full service salon here. Any thing any of you ladies want to have done, we can do. Let me call the manageress now, so she can have her staff available within, say two hours."

Chapter 28

By the time two hours had passed, each one of the women had selected two formal costumes. Mary also had several casual outfits, Erin and Johnica each had selected some slacks and shirts they could mis and match, and Fiona had three pairs of jeans of various colors, sweaters, and a daring cami-top that showed her bare arms. As she had never bared her arms in her adult life, or worn jeans since she was a teenager, she felt like a kid in a candy shop.

Mary and Johnica sat with Mrs. George, enjoying a cup of tea, while the stylists worked their magic on Erin and Fiona. Fiona had finally decided to have her long hair cut very short, with just barely enough to allow it to curl naturally. After much discussion and visualization with the computer aided stylist, Fiona' hair was lightened, and red highlights run throughout. By the time she was done, her fair was combed into a natural, puffy Marcel wave. Erin had a trim, to shoulder length, but had the top layered severely. In a rare moment of weakness, she let the colorist talk her into a frost and tip.

When it was Mary and Johnica's turn, Johnica knew exactly what she wanted. A very short, almost mannish cut, with the top permed to a tight curl. Mary was still undecided. She sat in the chair, spun her back to the mirror, told the stylist, "Do what ever you think will work; I don't want to see it till you're done. Do anything you want, short of shaving my head. Oh, and no little old lady blue hair, okay?"

Mrs. George called for more tea for Erin and Fiona, then came over to the styling chair where Mary was sitting. "Madam," the colorist asked, "what was your hair color before you went gray? I thought, perhaps, to give you a lighter shade of your natural color. Would that suit?"

"I told you to do whatever you thought best, but I don't know about a different color. I've been gray for so long, I'm used to it."

"Betty," Mrs. George said, "please use the computer to show Mrs. Finestre how she'd look with very light auburn hair. I take it, Madam, your hair was very red in your youth?"

Mary laughed. "Oh, yes, Mrs. George, VERY red indeed. As I got older and the gray crept in, it got lighter until it appeared pink. Then one morning I woke up and it had all gone gray."

"Yes, Betty, I think a very light auburn would suit Madam very well. Perhaps with some darker highlights. What do you think?"

When Betty had Mary's image up on the monitor, with her hair in a short bob, with the suggested colors in place, Mary called The other women over for their opinion. Erin said, "Ma, that looks like your wedding picture. You've got to do it."

Mary finally agreed, on the condition that she didn't have to look until Betty and the colorist and the stylist were completely finished.

By the time Mary and Johnica were finished in the salon, it was almost 5:30. Mrs. George led the group back to Ladies Furnishing, so they could change into one of the casual outfits they had chosen. While they were in the fitting rooms, Mrs. George had her assistant call Major Williams for the transport vehicle, and left instructions with him that the ladies' parcels would be delivered to them at 10:00 the next morning.

A large Bentley awaited them at curb side when they emerged from the store. Mary went directly to the car and ran her hand over the highly polished blue finish. The driver, a young woman in livery wearing the insignia of the Duke of Argyle on her cap, came round to open the rear door for Mary. Before Mary could bring herself to get in, she ran her hand one more time over the paint job, then reverently touched the carpet and leather upholstery. After she had climbed in, Erin and Fiona went next, taking the rearward facing seat, and Johnica sat next to her mother-in-law.

"Ladies," the chauffeur said through the intercom, "I've instructions to take you to meet your family at the Hotel Intercontinental. Does that meet with your approval, or have you somewhere else you'd like to go first?"

"Would it be possible to stop at a market somewhere, "Mary asked.

"I take it you're Mrs. Finestre? Your husband asked that you not stop to shop for food on the way back, as he had taken care of that."

"Well, in that case, I suppose you may as well take up to the Intercontinental," Mary said. Turning to Johnica, Mary grumbled, "I can imagine what that lot bought. Two six packs of beer apiece, and a jumbo bag of cheese curls."

Erin laughed, "Not if Neal had anything to say about it. He'd go for Cheez Wiz and crackers. And he'd rather have a giant bottle of cola, if he could get it. But I suppose sugar is rationed here just like back home."

No one saw the chauffeur's smile.

Chapter 29

Pulling up in front of the Hotel Intercontinental, the women couldn't get over the sheer sumptuousness of the facility. Nothing they had seen in recent years could compare to this, especially nothing for non-governmental employees. They were greeted by a liveried doorman, who escorted them to the head bellman, who in turn took them to the front desk. The concierge greeted them effusively, and presented the bellman keys to their rooms.

When Mary, Fiona, Erin and Johnica were in the lift with the bellman, Fiona asked, "Did we really get the whole floor to ourselves?"

The bellman smiled patiently. "Yes, Miss. We have explicit instructions from Major Williams. No one but hand picked members of the staff are to be allowed on the third floor. Oh, and the second and fourth floors are empty, with the exception of several members of His Grace's personal staff, who are assigned to you as guides and assistants."

"Don't you mean as guards?" Johnica asked.

"No, Madam, not at all. We have emptied the floors above and below you for security purposes, but only to protect you, not to keep you here. You are, of course, free to come and go as you please. His Grace has simply assigned some of his people to help. For instance, two of his young ladies are, even now, caring for the two young gentlemen in your party. And, Miss," he said to Fiona, "your young man is waiting with your brothers and sister to go to a club, if that's acceptable. As London is a very old city, it can be difficult to navigate your first time out, so there are two people available to get you there and back. But don't worry," he added with a wink, "they're not chaperones."

Fiona sputtered. She had never really been allowed to date. Not that her parents objected, but the laws were so stringent, she had more fun sitting home with her brothers and Meghan playing old board games than she could have at an "official matchmaking gathering." Mary just put her arms around Fiona and told her she should have fun, then whispered in her ear that if she wanted to have a talk before she went out to come over.

When they reached the third floor, the bellman directed Mary to the door at the far end of the hall. When he pushed the door open, Mary thought she was in heaven. In the center of a large room, furnished with Queen Ann settees and cherry wood tables, stood her husband dressed in a brocade dressing gown and satin pajamas. Next to John was an orgy of sweets: chocolate faerie cakes, petit fours, creme tarts, and an ice bucket containing not champagne but a quart of ice cream. Mary went to John and kissed him quite soundly. She asked, "Would you mind if Fiona and I had a little talk first? She and Austin have a date, and she's never been out with a man."

John left Mary and Fiona in the parlor, while he went to the bedroom. Mary could hear the television come on, and was surprised to hear the language allowed on the BBC. "Fiona, sit down for a minute, and lets talk."

"Granny, I don't know what to expect with Austin. You know I've never really been out with anyone. What if he want's to kiss me. Should I let him?"

"Honey, you're 25 years old. You're old enough to make you own mind up about these things. All I can tell you is if you feel like its right, it is. Just don't let him rush you into anything you don't feel ready for."

"But what if he wants more than just a kiss? And what if I want him to do more? I mean, I know about the birds and bees, I just don't know how all that buzzing applies to me and Austin."

"The best advice I can give you is don't rush anything. If it seems right tonight, it will be even more right tomorrow.

And if it's not right tonight, it was wrong to begin with. The only thing I ask is that you make Austin use some kind of protection. If you ask your guides, I'm sure one of them can tell you if condoms are available here. And if there's nothing you can use for protection, just make certain you're ready for the responsibility of a child before you commit to anything.

Fiona hugged her grandmother hard, and ran to meet the bellman in the hallway so he could show her to her room. Mary called out, "It's safe now John; come on out."

John kissed his wife again. "Don't worry about Fiona. I already had the "talk" with Austin. It seems he's also a virgin. But I did make the driver stop at the Boots chemist shop. I took him shopping for contraceptives. You know, it's amazing how far civilization's come without the assistance of the U.S."

"Oh, John. I can imagine that conversation in front of Jimmy and Neal. That's their little girl you two were discussing."

"I know. That's why I took Austin into another department while the two daddies were shopping for mourning suits."

"Mourning suits?" Mary asked.

"You know, those swallow tailed gray coats with the striped trousers, top hat and cravat? I was told they were *de rigeur* for royal audiences. You women have to where formal attire, but the men can get away without tuxedos because it's before 5:00 p.m."

"Alright, John," Mary said, "now that we've solved your sartorial requirements for the audience, would you care to explain this," gesturing to the collection of goodies.

"Well," said John, as he took his wife in his arms and fed her a bite of petit four, "we all decided to bring you something you couldn't get at home. I know your penchant for sweets. Neal and Jimmy each brought something home, too."

Mary laughed. "Erin said Neal would get Cheez Wiz

and crackers. What did he wind up with?"

"Well, he did get cheese, but not the squirty kind. He managed to get a small wheel of double cream brie, some Stilton and a bit of cheddar. He also got some of the prettiest fruit I've seen in years. He found apples from New Zealand, melons from Spain and grapes from South Africa. Oh, and he got a half-dozen bottles of white lambrusco to go with the cheese and fruit."

"I'm afraid to ask what Jimmy got."

"Do you really want to know?" At her nod, he continued, "I saw him pick out two dozen fresh oysters, some kind of crab, sausage he had cooked at the market, and I think he may have a couple baked potatoes thrown in for good measure. But I think I know what his plans are for tonight. The first thing he wanted to know was if they had their own room, and could somebody watch the kids."

Mary took a swipe of frosting off one of the faerie cakes and fed it to John. "I think you and Neal had the exact same thing in mind. You just know what works best as an aphrodisiac with your own wife."

John made a great show of licking frosting from Mary's hand. "Alright now, wife. What do you say we put this wheeled cart to good use?"

"Why, Mr. Finestre, whatever do you mean? Surely you don't think that cart would support anything heavier than the food already on it. An I for one don't intend to waste all those luscious treats."

"What I meant was we could take the cart into the bedroom. You see, there's a television there, with four channels that are not controlled by the government. It's wonderful, and there's commercials and frontal nudity and everything. I thought we could become titillated watching the suggestive programming on ITV and feed each other some of that double chocolate and caramel ice cream before it all melts.

Unless of course you'd like me to try to lick it off you. Just say the word, your wish is my command."

Mary took hold of the trolley handle and pushed it towards the bedroom. "I wouldn't think of wasting perfectly good ice cream like that. Besides, it's way too cold. Now, frosting, that's another matter."

Chapter 30

The entire group gathered in John and Mary's sitting room for breakfast the next morning. Three waiters brought in two trolleys each, laden with huge quantities of food. Faced with their first "Full English Breakfast," Meghan and Fiona kept looking around for the diet police. They were served both coffee and tea, available with copious amounts of sugar and cream, sausage, bacon, ham, fried eggs, toast, sliced tomatoes and baked beans. When Rose Whittier, one of the guides provided by the Duke, knocked at the door, John admitted her and asked, "When is everyone else coming to join us for breakfast? There's enough food here for the entire hotel."

"No, no, Mr. Finestre. That's just an English Breakfast. You'll find the same fare at restaurants and pubs all over the country. Don't you care for this type of food? I took the liberty of ordering for you this morning. If you'd prefer something else, I'll be more than happy to see to it."

"Do you mean to say," Mary asked, "that this food is all for us? Isn't there a fat quota specified by the health department here? And isn't sugar rationed?"

"Rationed? Oh, no, Mrs. Finestre. Nothing has been rationed here, other than petrol in the 1970's, since 1954. Don't tell me you still have rationing in the States."

"Not still," Johnica answered. "We have rationing again. In the last three or four years, the government has begun limiting individual's intake of sugar and fat. There are limits in restaurants how much fat and simple carbohydrates are in each serving. If a kitchen is caught with dishes in excess, the business risks being fined, and the chef can be jailed."

Ms. Whittier was taken aback at the description of their home country. "Well, when you're done, I'd like to review your itinerary for today."

The Callahan's took their plates and dug into the

breakfast with abandon. Austin told John he hadn't eaten this well since before his grandmother had died. Everyone agreed that it was all marvelous.

Ms. Whittier poured herself a cup of tea and took a seat opposite John and Mary. "Mrs. Finestre," she said, "do you suppose when you and Mr. Finestre are through with breakfast I could speak with the two of you privately? There are some things regarding your situation I need to review for his Grace."

"Certainly, Ms. Whittier," Mary said. "That would be fine. There are some things I'd like to go over with you as well."

When every one was done breakfast, including three cups of heavily sugared coffee each, everyone except John and Mary went with Mr. Sullivan, one of the guides assigned to them. They were scheduled to visit Madame Tousaud's and, if there was time before dinner, the Old Bailey. Mary was surprised to see Mr. Sullivan make an overt pass at Austin. She told herself to ask about this later, as well.

"Well, Ms. Whittier," John said, "we've finally gotten rid to all of them. Now, what was it you wanted to discuss?"

"His Grace, the Duke of Argyle, has asked that I try to ascertain you frame of mind and your personal opinions regarding certain areas. Would that be acceptable?"

Mary looked at John and nodded. "I don't see a problem," John answered. "We don't have anything to hide that I know of."

"His Grace wants to know exactly what goes on onboard the Shuttle from which you escaped, and what we can expect to happen when the passengers arrive at Skylab 6. Do you have any information you can share on these points?"

"Well, on the Shuttle," Mary told her, "it's pretty much as you would expect for any long trip. Oh, except there are armed guards, and the cabin stewards pass out tranquilizers and sleeping pills in addition to making up the bunks for the evening."

"There was one incident," John took up the story. "It's the one that got us busted to begin with. Are you familiar with that awful national anthem the president has authorized?"

"New anthem? Why no, the only one we ever heard was the Star Spangled Banner."

"Oh, you've heard this one before," Mary said. "I know you're not old enough to remember, but surely you're familiar with Handel's Largo. It is sung at all the EU openings, or at least it was until ten years ago. I don't know what they do now. Well, back before John and I were born, it was also the anthem of Nazi Germany, Deutschland Uber Alles. They've given it some insipid lyrics on the pretense that it's easier to sing than the one by Francis Scott Key."

John took over. "The first full night out, after all the passengers had assembled in the dining room, the anthem was played. Naturally, everyone rose and most began to sing. All except a very drunken retired military man, named Joel Meirhoff. He spent quite a bit of his career in Germany, so he was familiar with the song's history. He began to sing, under the English lyrics, the German words. Rather than let him be taken out by the security guards, Mary and I led an insurrection of sorts."

"You didn't start a riot or anything, did you?"

Mary laughed, "Oh, no. This fine, brave gentleman, here," she patted John's leg, "began to sing the Star Spangled Banner." I joined him, then almost everyone else joined in. It was a blast!"

Ms. Whittier laughed with them. "Oh, my, Mr. Finestre. That's just like that scene from that old Claude Rains and Paul Henried movie."

Mary asked John, "Claude Rains and Paul Henried? Oh, yes, Claude Rains played the prefect of police and Paul Henried was married to Ingrid Bergman. You mean

'Casablanca." We always refer to it as the Humphry Bogart movie, though. But I'm surprised you've seen that film. At home, any depictions of war, insurrection or sex are strictly forbidden."

"You don't mean to tell me you still have censorship? I always thought America was such a progressive country."

"We were progressive," John told her disgustedly, "until about ten or twelve years ago, anyway. Then, in the presidential election, not only was an extreme right-wing Republican elected, but almost the entire House and Senate were Republican, too. They began to pass more and more legislation to restrict our personal liberties. Eventually, it got so bad you couldn't live or work where you wanted. You when where you were told. If a person refused to remove themselves from a home on the government's directive, the resident was forcibly removed, and frequently sent to an institution for the mentally ill. The rationale was that if you disobeyed the government, you must be crazy, therefore you had no rights to possess property of any kind. And if you refused to vacate a situation in favor of an appointee of the regime, you were also considered too mad to hold a job."

Mary took up the story. "There were also homes for the elderly. Not nursing homes, as we used to have, or even assisted living situations, but single room billets. I always called them warehouses. And when you get tired of living for your next bowl of oatmeal. You get the option of taking a 70+."

"70+?" Ms. Whittier asked. "What on earth is that?"

"70+ is a the governmental euphemism for a Potassium Cyanide capsule. I understand it's extremely effective in controlling unwanted population."

"Mr. Finestre, how large a security staff is assigned to the Elder Shuttle? And how large a crew is assigned to it?"

"Let's see, there were eighteen passenger cars, each with two security officers assigned. The crew had three cars, with, oh, I'd say around twenty crew members, making a total of sixty sis staff members and around eighty passengers. What's that total, one hundred, forty six? Would you say that's right, Mary?"

"I think so. Ms. Whittier, why this interest in the staffing requirements and conditions on the Shuttle?"

"I'm terribly sorry. I do have strict instructions from His Grace not to divulge anything as yet. Now then, can I interest the two of you in a tour of our fair city?"

Ms. Whittier, would you mind if I spoke with my husband for just a few moments?"

"No, certainly no. Would you like me to wait outside?"

"No, I don't think that's necessary. We'll just step into the other room for a moment."

"Mary took John by the hand and led him into the bedroom. John grinned at her and said, "I don't think this is really proper, my dear. Leaving a guest in our parlor while you drag me into your boudoir to have your way with me."

"Listen to who's talking. Aren't you the one who tried to throw the guests out of our wedding just a few days ago so you could 'get to the good stuff' I think you said. Anyway, that's what I wanted to talk to you about."

"The 'good stuff?' By all means, but I still think we need to get rid of the woman in the next room.

Mary was becoming exasperated. "No, you big oaf. I was talking about our wedding. Would you mind if we did it again? I mean, I know we're married and everything, but I think it would mean a lot to my family if they could actually take part in the ceremony. And I don't know about you, but I'd really prefer to be married by a priest. Oh, and do you realize we don't have a certificate or anything to prove we're really married. Why, if we had a baby, he'd be illegitimate."

"No, he wouldn't," John said with a laugh. "I'd make sure the little beggar knew how to read. If you want to get married again, my love, I'm all for it."

"If you'd rather wait until you're family can be with us, too, I understand. I really don't mind waiting."

"Mary, I told you, I had two boys. You know men are not as sentimental about these things as women. And besides, they are really close to their mother, and I'm afraid there would be some hard feelings from them. Lets do it, and I'll send them pictures as soon as I'm able."

Mary kissed him, and John was hard pressed not to take her to bed right then. When she broke away, he took her by the hand and led her back into the parlor. "Ms. Whittier, are there still Catholic churches in England?"

"Of course, Mr. Finestre. We've had religious suffrage since Charles II. Why do you ask?"

"Well," John answered as he drew Mary to his side, "this lovely lady does me the honor of marrying me all over agin in a religious ceremony. You see, we were married by the captain of the Elder Shuttle. We have no marriage certificate, and it means a lot to Mary's family to take part in something of this magnitude. And besides, it seems a shame to waste that mourning coat and not get married."

Chapter 31

By the time Mr. Sullivan had returned with his charges, it was 2:00 p.m. and Ms. Whittier had most of the plans set with Mary and John. She had located a Catholic church that met with their approval, and had made arrangements with the priest to perform a nuptial mass.

Mary told John she wanted to break the news to her family herself. John excused himself when everyone was through with their tea, and went into the bedroom. Mary said, "Fiona, have you ever been a maid of honor?"

"A maid of honor? No, Granny, none of my close friends are married. Why."

"Because John and I are going to renew our vows at St. John the Lesser Church this evening, and we wanted you to be my maid of honor, since without you, we never would have met, and none of this would have happened. Of course, we want everyone else to take part, too."

When the family had quieted down again, Erin said, "Ma, you know you don't have to do this just for us."

"Oh, I know, and it's up to you whether or not you want to actually stand up with us or sit in the pews. But we wanted to actually have a mass again."

Austin asked, "A mass. You mean an Anglican mass?"

"No, Austin, a real, honest to God Catholic mass, with a priest and church and everything. Well, what do you say?"

Immediately, the women gathered around Mary and began to discuss plans. Mary called over their voices, "Why don't you guys go sit with John in the bedroom. We'll call you when we're through."

A knock sounded at the door. "I'll answer that," Ms. Whittier said.

The Duke of Argyle waited outside with Mrs. George from the department store, who carried several dress bags. Ms.

Whittier stepped aside to admit them. "Your grace, this is a surprise," Ms. Whittier said.

"When you called me this afternoon and told me of Mrs. Finestre's plans," the Duke said, "I felt I had to make a contribution. Mrs. George, if you would be so kind."

Mrs. George stepped past the Duke, and laid the garment bags across the back of the sofa. "Mrs. Finestre, His Grace called me this morning when he received the news, and had me assemble some things for the wedding party. Of course we had your sizes on file, so there wasn't any problem."

"I had thought to wear that lovely green silk I picked out yesterday," Mary said, still puzzled, but dying to know what was in the garment bags.

"Well, I know how much you liked the style of that outfit, so I've taken the liberty of selecting another of a similar style, as well as complementary garments for what His Grace assumed would be the rest of the wedding party. Of course, if these don't meet with your approval, I can call out for something else to be sent round."

"Oh, Ma," Erin said, "lets at least look at what Mrs. George brought."

It really didn't take much convincing. "Okay, lets see," Mary laughed. She really felt like a little girl on her birthday. Inside the first bag was an outfit made along the same lines as the green silk, but the similarity stopped there.

Mary held up a pair of silver-gray silk trousers. They were so soft to the touch, she had to hold them a moment to make sure she wasn't dreaming. Removing the tissue from the next hanger, she found a long camisole that would fall to her knees of the same material. Under the camisole was another tissue. When Mary tore that away, Erin gasped out loud. Mary lifted out a silver lace coat that would sweep the floor. There were tiny points of gold embroidered over the lace all down the front placket and around the neckline.

Mary had to stop to wipe away a tear. "Your Grace, this is entirely unexpected."

"Nonsense, Mrs. Finestre. I wanted to give you something nice as a wedding gift. Why not your wedding dress. Oh, and don't you dare try to curtsey again. We haven't done that here since Grandmum died."

"Yes, Your Grace," Mary said. "Mrs. George, would you please assist me in opening the rest of these things."

Mrs. George did have exquisite taste. She had chosen outfits made from the same pattern for the other women, but in a rainbow of colors. In place of the embroidered lace coat, these were made of sheer gauze, in a slightly darker color than the trousers. From beneath the final package, Mary saw Mrs. George extract a long flat box she hadn't noticed before under the bags. "Your Grace, this is the other item you requested."

"Thank you, Mrs. George. Mrs. Finestre, where would I find your husband?"

"Through that door, Your Grace," Mary Said, puzzled as he went into the bedroom to join the other men.

"Alright, ladies, we haven't much time," Ms. Whittier announced. Let's all go down the hall to Mrs. Callahan's room and get you dressed, then we can come back to join the gentlemen and be on our way to church."

When everyone was dressed and had repaired hair and makeup with the help of Mrs. George, they returned to the Finestre's parlor. Ms. Whittier looked in the bedroom and found it empty. She called down to the desk to see of any messages had been left. She smiled as she hung up the phone. "Mrs. Finestre, His Grace has taken the gentlemen on to the church, and they will meet us there. Shall we go?"

The six women rode down in the lift to the ground floor, and were escorted by the bellman through the lobby to the door, where the doorman handed them into the limousine the Duke had provided. The same driver was standing at the open door who had taken them from the store yesterday. She was all smiles.

As few minutes later, they arrived at St. John the Lesser. Mary wondered at all the cars outside, and asked Ms. Whittier what was going on.

Well, Mrs. Finestre, I hope you won't object, but I believe His Grace invited a few members of the government to attend, so they could meet you and Mr. Finestre."

Mary looked at trifle bewildered. "Well, I suppose that's all right. I was really only expecting an intimate family affair."

When the women entered the vestibule, Mary couldn't resist opening the door a crack and peeking inside. There were yellow roses with silver ribbons festooning every third pew. There appeared to be nearly fifty people in attendance. A man standing near the altar saw her peeking, and rushed back to the vestibule. Mary noticed a camera bag slung over his shoulder.

"Mrs. Finestre," he said, slightly out of breath, "I am Robin Spencer. Harry...I mean His Grace, and I are third cousins. When he told me about your plans today, I felt it imperative to commemorate the ceremony photographically. I promise to be discreet, and thoroughly unobtrusive. You won't even know I'm here. When you are ready, Rose," he said, turning to Ms. Whittier, "just press that buzzer next to the door. It's the signal for the gentlemen."

They watched as he walked up the aisle. Just before the door closed, Mary thought she saw him bend down to speak to someone. Moments later, the door opened again, and a lovely young Indian woman entered, carrying something made of cloth.

"Ms. Whittier," the Indian woman said, "would you make me known to the bride?"

"Certainly, Madame Prime Minister. Ms. Narwahli, may I present to you the bride, Mrs. John Finestre, her daughter,

Erin Mulroney, Mrs. Mulroney's daughters Fiona and Meghan, and Mrs. Finestre's daughter-in-law, Johnica Callahan."

Ms. Narwahli greeted each of the wedding party with a nod and a smile, then walked over to stand in front of Mary. "Mrs. Finestre, I was told you had taken a great liking to my mode of dress. I am very well pleased, and may I say it suits you tremendously well. I have brought you a small token, something I hope you will wear today." Ms. Narwahli held out the cloth wrapped package to Ms. Whittier, who took it from her with both hands and offered it for Mary to open.

As Mary parted the cloth, she inhaled a sharp breath. Inside the plain parcel was a gorgeous swath of fabric of silver tissue. "Madame Prime Minister, I don't know what to say. This is exquisite." Mary wiped tears from her eyes for the second time that day. "I'm terribly sorry, but I find myself without either tissue or purse. Could one of you ladies possibly spare one?"

Ms. Narwahli smiled at Mary and produced a small square of cotton and lace. "I know it's rather old fashioned, but my grandmother insisted I carry one. It's been a habit I'm afraid I've never outgrown."

Mary used the handkerchief to wiper her eyes. "I'm sorry to be such an old fool, Ms. Narwahli. I'll return this to you tomorrow. Now then, would you mind showing me how best to wear this?"

Taking the veil from Mary, Ms. Narwahli caught it at the halfway point , made a quick estimation and laid it gently over Mary's head. Throwing the end over Mary's shoulder, she then adjusted the fabric until it hung to the hem of her lace coat, both front and back. The silver tissue exactly matched the silk of the trousers and camisole. Ms. Narwahli stepped in front of Mary again and gave her a quick hug. "That's for luck," she smiled, then returned to the nave of the church.

Mary wiped her eyes again, then said to Ms. Whittier,

"Well, now. If I hope to get through this without completely breaking down, we'd best get on with it. Will you press the buzzer please?"

"Certainly, Mrs. Finestre. But your husband asked if we could do things a little differently today. When I press the buzzer, Mr. Mulroney, Master Sean and Master Robert will join us. Then you may proceed down the aisle."

This time, Mary had to wipe her nose as well as her eyes. Ms. Whittier pressed the buzzer, and moments later the door opened and Neal, Sean and Robert stepped through. Mary noticed that while they did indeed wear their mourning suits, someone had taken the time to provide them with cravats in the color to match the outfit of the lady each would be escorting. Each of the men carried bouquets of three yellow rouses tied with silver, which they handed to their lady. Neal presented the fourth to Fiona. They were finally ready.

Erin stood with her son, Sean, Meghan with her cousin Robert, Johnica with her husband, and Fiona stood alone as the maid of honor. Mary heard the organ playing Mozart's "Wedding March" from *le Nozze di Figaro*. Just before Sean opened the door, Ms. Whittier stepped out though a side door, and came back with a bouquet of yellow and red roses which she handed to Mary.

As they walked down the aisle, Mary was hard pressed not to just break down and cry openly. She know John loved her, but she never knew he would go to such lengths to show the world how much. She saw John and Jimmy waiting for them at the altar, with young Jamison holding a pillow next to his uncle. Mary smiled at the sight of the ten year old. Someone had managed to dress him in an Eaton collared shirt, jacket and short pants with knee socks. She knew he was mortified, but she thought he just looked so damned cute.

As they reached the altar, the men stepped to the right and the women to the left. Mary was surprised they were working so well without rehearsal. When Mary finally reached the bottom step, John reached down to take her hand and lifted her up to him. He whispered to her, "you are so lovely. If you'd let me, I'd do this one a month."

She just smiled at him. She knew she'd never get a word out without crying, and worried she'd never get through the vows. The priest took his place at the altar rail. When Mary looked at him, she couldn't help smiling her delight. Next to the priest, she saw Austin Fitzhugh wearing the alb of an altar boy, prepared to help serve the nuptial mass. The priest began the ceremony, and Mary was surprised that the traditional vows hadn't been changed. With the exception of the omission of the word "obey," it was exactly the same words she had recited with her first husband all those years ago. When the priest got to the blessing of the rings, Mary whispered, "I'm sorry, Father, we don't have any."

The good father just smiled at her benevolently and motioned young Jamison forward. Mary saw Jamison was carrying a silver velvet pillow, with a small box in the center. Jamison held the cushion up to the priest, who removed the box, opened it and extracted two white gold rings and placed them on a tray Austin held out to him. Mary couldn't quite make out the design through her tears, but she saw they were white gold, and there was an emerald in one of them. Even when John placed the ring on her finger, the only thing of which she was certain was a heart shaped emerald, but even that looked rather watery and wavy. As she picked John's ring from the salver and placed it on his finger, she felt some engraving worked into a design. Right then, she decided she'd examine both later.

When the ceremony concluded, Robert and Jamison came forward to the foot of the altar steps and placed two yellow-draped chairs for John and Mary. John seated his bride first, then took the seat to her right. He held her hand throughout the mass, even when they were called upon to kneel. It was as if he was afraid to let go of her. Mary was glad, as she wasn't about to let this one get away, either.

When the mass ended and the chairs removed, the priest stood before them for a final blessing. The pipe organ roared to life with Handel's "And the Trumpets Shall Sound," and John turned his wife and started down the aisle towards the door. He let go of her hand long enough to place his right arm around her waist and take her left hand in his.

The entire family assembled in the vestibule, and formed a receiving line. The priest greeted Mary and John both with a hug and took his place at the end of the line. Austin shook John's hand and gave Mary a hug and a kiss on the cheek. She said, "Austin, I was surprised to see you as an altar boy."

He smiled at her. "I wanted to give you something special. This was the best thing I could think of. And besides, I haven't served in ten years, and I sort of missed it. You didn't mind, did you?"

"Not at all. This doesn't mean you want to be a priest, does it?"

Austin laughed as he slipped in beside Fiona and gently took her hand. "Not hardly. I've found out I like girls."

The first guests to leave the nave were the Duke of Argyle and the Prime Minister. As John shook the Duke's hand, he said, "Harry, I can't thank you enough. This is a day I'll remember for the rest of my life. And Ms. Narwahli, it's been a pleasure to have you here to share our day."

Mary was surprised John knew Ms. Narwahli, but then decided he had been at the church for a while and the Duke had introduced them. The Duke leaned over to kiss Mary's cheek. "Mrs. Finestre, I've taken the liberty of securing the ballroom at your hotel for several hours for a small reception. After all, we can't have a wedding without a meal afterwards, now can we?"

Mary thanked him, and turned to greet the rest of her guests, thankful that Ms. Whittier was now standing behind them making introductions. When it was finally time to leave, everyone but the bride and groom went out onto the steps and walkway of the church. Mary said, "when I get you home, Gianni Finestre, you've got some explaining to do. You can start with why you called the Duke of Argyle 'Harry' and finish where these rings came from. But not now. First, I want to go out there and climb back into that Bentley."

"I'm sorry to disappoint you, my love, but we won't be riding back in the Bentley.

Mary just looked at him as he led her out onto the front steps. She gasped when she saw their conveyance at the curb. A horse-drawn coach, with glass windows all round and driver and footmen in the livery of Argyle. Four gray horses were in the traces. Mary kissed her husband again, much more soundly than she dared in church, while her family applauded. Just before she let John hand her up into the equipage, she turned to the crowd and gently tossed the bouquet directly to Fiona.

Chapter 32

John asked the coachman to take several turns through Hyde Park before returning them to the hotel. He didn't give Mary time to ask any of the questions she was itching to ask, as he kept her busy fending off his hands so they could wave to passerby, including those on horseback who could easily see into the windows. While Mary loved her new husband dearly, she was not anxious to give London a show.

By the time they arrived at the hotel, their reception was underway. The head table awaited them, with Mary's family, Austin and the priest already seated. A sextet which included a french horn and harpsichord was playing quietly in the background. When John led Mary into the ballroom, the entire assembled group stood and applauded. He smiled and waved his best royal wave at the crowd, while pulling Mary behind him towards the dais. She whispered to him as he handed her into her chair, "You're not off the hook yet, Finestre. I still want answers." She smiled and waved at the crowd.

John took his seat beside her. "All in good time, my love. All in good time. Let's enjoy the food Ms. Whittier has arranged, then I'll do my best to satisfy you. Curiosity and otherwise," he said with a leer.

Mary couldn't help but laugh at his lascivious look and raised eyebrows. A waiter came behind Mary to fill her champagne glass, then filled John's. Mary turned to the waiter just before he left. "Young man, after this glass is finished, do you think you could replace it with some of that lovely cider I tasted today?"

The waiter beamed at her as if she had just discovered a national treasure. "Certainly, Madam. And would Madam care for anything else?"

"No, I believe that will be sufficient," Mary said.

The waiter leaned over and whispered something to

John. John laughed and just shook his head no. Mary asked, "And what was that all about?"

John was still laughing when he answered, "He wanted to know if he could bring me a pint of good English beer, since he had to go next door for your cider."

Mary couldn't help but laugh with him. The waiter returned a few minutes with another champagne glass, this one filled. He placed it in front of Mary, who took a tentative sip. When she tasted the bite of the drought cider, she nodded as if she had just approved a newly opened bottle of wine, and thanked the waiter profusely. She said to John, "I feel so bad, we have nothing to tip these people with. I wish there was something we could do in return for them."

"That's something Harry and I need to talk to you about later," he said enigmatically.

Mary soon realized her husband was not going to tell her anything until he was good and ready, and gave up for the time being. Course followed course, and as the meal would down, she was beginning to feel as if she was 169 instead of her actual age. She said to Fiona, who sat to her right, "I'm getting too damned old for this nonsense. I mean, the honeymoon is bad enough, but I don't know if I can live through the reception."

Fiona laughed and motioned to her uncle, who was sitting next to John, and watching the exchange between his niece and mother. Jimmy stood, and tapped on his glass with the handle of his knife. He said, very carefully, just as he had practiced, "My Lords, Ladies and Gentlemen, I'd like to thank you for your attendance at my mother's and her husband's renewal of vows. It means a lot to us, and to them, I am sure, that you cared enough about them to share this special day. Now, to the bride and groom: I won't offer you the traditional toast, about kids and things. I can't imagine you presenting Fiona with a brand new baby uncle in nine months." He waited until the laughter stopped. "Therefore, I'd like to offer you an old Gaelic toast. John, I'll let Ma translate it to the original for you. I never could get my tongue around all those consonants. 'May those that love you, love you. Those that hate you, may the Lord turn their hearts. And if He cannot turn their hearts, may He turn their ankles, so you may know them by their limping.'"

The entire assembly laughed, and offered their glasses to salute. Dessert was served. Mary was delighted to find it was a trifle, instead of the traditional dry, over-decorated tiered wedding cake. The waiter rolled a trolley first to Mary and John, and served them before anyone else at the head table. After thanking the waiter profusely, she took her first bite of the lush, decadent dessert. Mary closed her eyes to savor the taste and texture, then whispered to John, "I don't know what exactly you have planned for this evening, but I think I may have just had an orgasm."

John told her, "Just make certain you save one or two for me. Here comes Harry, don't have one now. I don't want to have to explain the noises you might make."

Mary almost choked on the bite she had just put in her mouth, and slapped John on the shoulder. The Duke said to her, "I hope the dessert is to your liking, Mrs. Finestre?"

John answered for her, just to have the last word, "Oh yes, she likes it very much. I think she may like it more than she likes me, for that matter."

Mary shot him "the look." She said, "At this moment, John, I like the trifle much better than I like you. You'll have to correct that later."

"Mrs. Finestre, after, when you've made the rounds of all the tables and greeted all your guests again, could you please join me in private. There are some thinks John and I would like to discuss with you. I've staked out the table in the rear of the hall, in the corner. I think we'll be rather unobtrusive there, and

I believe young Mr. Fitzhugh can keep an eye on the room to make certain we're not disturbed."

"Certainly, Your Grace. That would be wonderful. There are quite a few things I'd like to speak to you about."

"Of course, Madam," the Duke said, as he bowed slightly and turned away.

"John, what is going on? When you and I first met, at the aerodrome, remember I told you I felt as if I had fallen down a rabbit hole? Well, it's getting curiouser and curiouser. First, we're swept away into the Elder-Shuttle. You and I meet, fall in love and get married before the second dinner is served onboard the Shuttle. We almost create a mutiny in an effort to protect a drunk. Then, of all things, I am reunited with my family and carried even further down the rabbit hole, into another country. A country where, not only do they not arrest us, but welcome us as if we were prodigal children. Something is going on, and I don't think it has anything to do with magic pills or drinks."

"There are some things I would rather let Harry explain to you Mary. I'm not trying to put you off, honestly. I'm not even clear on some of the things, myself. Let's just wait until things settle down a bit, then we'll both talk to Harry and straighten things out."

"That's something else, John. Why all of a sudden are you calling the Duke of Argyle "Harry?"

"Because he asked me to. There is one thing I want to tell you before we go to meet him. While you ladies were going over dresses, Harry brought a wooden box into the bedroom. He actually gave me a choice of rings for both of us. I tried to refuse, as they were all far out of my reach. Harry insisted, saying the rings were his to give away as he chose. After I talked it over with Jimmy, I picked these two." John took her left hand and held it up next to his. Mary finally got her first good look at their wedding rings.

146

John's ring did indeed have engraving all around the band. Turning it, Mary saw what she took to be a shamrock, a thistle, a rose and a daffodil. In the center of each bloom was a stone. She asked John to take it off so she could have a closer look. In the daffodil was a citrine, a garnet in the rose, amethyst in the thistle and an emerald set in the shamrock. John said, "Each flower represents one of the Kingdoms of Great Britain. I thought it appropriate as it was Britain making all this possible. Now, let's look at yours."

Mary's ring consisted of a heart-shaped emerald, set withing the hands and crown of the *cladagh*. The flowers of the realm were likewise worked around the band. Slipping the ring from her finger, she looked inside. There she saw the words, *Ubi bene, ibi patria*. She thought, then asked John exactly what they meant.

"This is something I asked Harry to have engraved inside. I thought it a little trite just to have our names inside. I mean, we know who we are. The Latin translates to 'where you are happy, there is your home.' My ring has the same motto, because whenever I'm with you, I'm happy. Therefore, I am home. And it here is to be home, it suits me just fine."

"*Ubi bene, ibi patria,*" Mary repeated. "Home is where the heart is. John Finestre, I never knew you were such a romantic."

"I never was before. You just seem to bring out the horny old man, I guess."

Mary looked around the banquet room and saw the guests were finishing their desserts. She told John they should begin to make the rounds before people started to get restless. After they had greeted and thanked everyone for coming, they managed to make their way to the back of the hall. Not only was the Duke of Argyle waiting for them, but Jimmy and Neal were there as well. Mary noticed Austin sitting with the rest of the family at a nearby table, obviously keeping an eye on the surroundings.

The men rose as Mary approached, and John handed her into her seat. "Mrs. Finestre, John, I'm glad you were able to join us. I've been having the most enlightening conversation with your son and son-in-law, Mrs. Finestre."

"Your Grace, don't you think it's time you called me by my given name?" Mary said.

"Certainly, Mary. But only on the condition that you call me Harry. So very few people do, at least to my face, and it becomes quite tiresome to be subject of constant deference and condescension. Sometimes, I'd just like someone to speak to me as if I were just another human being. I mean, that's really what I am, save for an accident of birth."

Mary nodded her assent. Harry went on, "Let me get right to the point of this meeting. I feel we are very secure here, as the only people in the room are other members of the government, all of them well trusted. The only reason I asked Mr. Fitzhugh to keep watch is to save us from being interrupted.

"For some time, we have heard whisperings of human rights violations taking place in the United States. But, as you know, there has been little or no communication between the U.S. and the outside world for the last ten years or so. And ever since Canada fell to your government, we've heard nothing at all. Until your craft landed at Heathrow, we've had no direct knowledge of what has been happening. But now, we find things are actually much worse than we ever expected.

"What I wold like to propose, to all of you, is that Mr. Finestre, Mr. Callahan and Mr. Mulroney take positions within our Ministry of Intelligence. We can certainly use your expertise, and I believe there is a position for Mrs. Finestre as well. I intend to explain things more fully tomorrow, after you've all had time to digest the information. But for the time being, please consider our offer. There will be substantial pay for all involved, as well as housing allotments. We will also help you find lodging and will provide the seed money to get you set up there.

"I realize this is all rather sudden. But just think about it. With your permission, I will meet you tomorrow at around 7:oo p.m. to take you all to dinner we can discuss it further then, and finalize our plans."

When Harry stood, the rest of the men rose as well. He took Mary's hand in farewell first, then shook hands with each of the men. When he left, thy sat down heavily.

"Well," Neal said, "that was a shock. We come here with the clothes on our backs, then all of a sudden, we have full wardrobes. Then, the next thing you know we're offered good jobs with full benefits and everything."

"Just as I said, John," Mary said. "Curiouser and Curiouser.

Chapter 33

The banquet hall finally emptied, leaving only the very tired wedding party. Mary was sitting sideways on her chair, leaning back against her husband, with her feet propped up on another chair. "You know, Ma," Jimmy said with a smile, 'that's not a real lady-like position."

"Just be glad I've only got my feet up on the chair. If I had my way, I would have left an hour ago and gone to bed."

John pushed her upright and turned her to face him. "Why didn't you tell me that an hour ago? Then I wouldn't have had to be polite to all those lords, ladies and gentlemen. We could have had a lot more fun without them."

Pulling off his cravat and opening his collar, Neal offered his hand to Erin. "Well, we don't have to stay and be polite to anybody. If anyone needs us, we're going to put Jimmy's boys to bed then head there ourselves. Good night everybody."

"Neal, don't worry about the boys." Johnica said. "I'll see to them. I think I'll go on upstairs myself."

The rest of the group drifted off, leaving the bride and groom alone. "You know," John said, "I think that's some kind of record. Not only have we been married twice in one week, but in the same week I have inherited two children and six grandchildren. I must say, it's a rather nice feeling."

Mary hugged him. "You know, I was really surprised how quickly they took to you. I expected a little hostility from Erin and Jimmy. But I guess after you set Jimmy back on his heels at the aerodrome, he knows you're okay."

John stood up. "I hope you know I'm okay, too."

"I think you're more than okay," Mary said as she slipped an arm around his waist. Together, they walked to the lift, to go to their suite.

In the morning, following breakfast, Mary, John, Erin,

Jimmy, Johnica and Neal were driven to Number Ten Downing Street. They were scheduled to meet with the Prime Minister and the Duke of Argyle, to discuss the Duke's plans for them. When they arrived, they were shown into a well-lit room, furnished with about a dozen leather club chairs, and a podium set at up at one end of the room. They took their chairs and were joined shortly by Ms. Narwahli and Harry Windsor, the Duke of Argyle. They all greeted each other, and took their seats again. Before they started, a cart was wheeled in, and coffee and tea were served.

"Now that we are all here," Ms. Narwahli told them, "I think it's about time you learned exactly why we welcomed you so quickly when you begged asylum."

John was the first to speak up. "Harry told us a little last night, Ms. Narwahli. How there has been little or no communication from the U.S. for quite a while and there are rumors of human rights violations. Is that it?"

"Yes, Mr. Finestre, that's exactly it. You see, since Canada lost it's home rule and was taken over by the government in Washington, we cannot learn anything regarding the conditions in your country. We hoped you could either dispel the ideas we had regarding these violations, or confirm them so we may attempt to right a great wrong."

"What can we help you with?" Jimmy asked. "This is something we can definitely confirm. Just ask my mother, my sister and my wife about the violations of the rights of women. They no longer have any choice about working after they have children; they have no choice about birth control, no control over their bodies at all. Why, recently there were ordinances passed in most major cities prohibiting women from cutting their hair."

Erin took up the conversation. "Our daughters would like to go out with young men their own age, on their own, or with other people their own age. They can't. There is a strict segregation of the sexes in all things, and the only time they are allowed to mix is at an officially sanctioned 'matchmaking party.'"

Jimmy said, "Fiona went to one of those once. They can't play music, since someone may want to dance. All you do is stand around and drink some really bad fruit punch and watch a bunch of guys watch the girls. I believe she only went once. It's no wonder this generation waits until they are thirty five to get married."

"Not having any legal birth control may have something to do with it," Mary put in. "Who in their right minds wants to get married at eighteen and have one pregnancy a year until you go through menopause or die?"

"Do you really mean," Ms. Narwahli asked, "there really is no type of birth control? Why, your country pioneered it, ever since Margaret Sanger. And is there no surgical intervention to stop continual pregnancy?"

"No, there isn't," Johnica answered. "About the time our youngest was two, right after Jimmy had his vasectomy, sterilization became illegal, as they claimed it circumvented the will of nature. Soon thereafter, all forms of birth control were outlawed, including condoms. Then they even passed laws against sex outside of marriage, unless of course you were male and could afford the high-priced government brothels."

"Do you mean to tell us," Harry asked, "that the United States Government operates as a procurator?"

"Oh, yes," John said. "And very expensive whore house they are, too. Only the best paid government officials can afford them. On occasion, a civilian will go, but usually because his family has saved up for quite a while to give him a fling."

"John," Harry asked, "can you tell us about the Elder Shuttle? I mean, how did you and Mary get tickets, that sort of thing?"

"Well, first off," John answered, "I was given my ticket as a retirement gift from my company. Mary got her's from her family, and we met at the customs gate. The treatment onboard isn't that bad. But we learned, and shared with Ms. Whittier, that those sent on the trip aren't expected to return."

"I know what you told Rose, now I want to hear it again. Why are all those people being taken to Skylab 6?"

John reiterated the story he had learned from Major Meirhoff. When he was done, he realized, this was the first time Johnica and Erin had heard the whole of it. He asked, "Are you two alright? I thought Neal and Jimmy would have told you about it."

Neal said, "I didn't even know everything. It just makes me so damned angry to think my own government could do something like this."

"Mr. Mulroney," Ms. Narwahli said in an attempt to calm him, "I think it ceased to be 'your government' about ten years ago."

John asked, "Ms. Narwahli, we've answered all your questions, now I think its your turn. What exactly does the British government have in mind for us to do? I mean, the last thing we expected was the offer of jobs and housing. The shock still hasn't worn off."

"What we expect from your group, Mr. Finestre," Ms. Narwahli answered, "is to first help us get all those people off Skylab 6, then we want you to assist in the overthrow of the United States Government."

Chapter 34

Several minutes of stunned silence followed Ms. Narwahli's announcement. Jimmy was the first to regain his equilibrium. He said, "Ms. Narwahli, what exactly do you mean you want us to help overthrow the United States Government? I don't like the current regime, but I don't think any of us are prepared for infiltration and sabotage, not to mention high treason."

Ms. Narwahli took a sip of her coffee. "I did not think you were, Mr. Callahan. What we had in mind was primarily a rescue operation for you and the co-pilot of your choice to return to the Elder Shuttle, and remove anyone who wishes to leave. Then we would like you to travel to the space station and assist those people in returning to Earth as well."

Neal shook his head. "I don't think the two of us can do that single-handed."

"We don't intend for you to," Harry said. "You will be in the first ship, which will dock with the shuttle. Among your crew of ten will be eight NATO commandos. Following your ship will be a convoy of battle cruisers, prepared to assist you in any way they can. We want you to dock first merely as a subterfuge."

John stood up. "Harry, before we go any further, I think my family needs to discuss this in private. Is there some place we can go, perhaps to the hotel, then meet with you later to iron out the details?"

"Certainly, John. I'll have the driver take you to the hotel."

"Really, Harry," Mary said, "if it's alright, I for one would rather walk, or even take the Tube. Could that be arranged?"

"Of course, Mary. I hadn't realized your view of London has been rather isolated since your arrival. Mr.

Sullivan is in the outer office. I would like it if he could act as your guide, but I promise he is only there to get you from place to place, not to see that you only come in contact with the correct people."

"Harry," John said, "that would be just fine."

They left by the back door of Ten Downing Street, and headed for the nearest Tube stop. Mary said to their escort, "Mr. Sullivan, could you please get us to a museum. I think my husband and I would like to spend a few hours just walking about."

"Certainly, Mrs. Finestre. Would the rest of you care to go to the Victoria and Albert as well, or would you prefer somewhere else?"

When the discussion was ended, the group decided to go separate directions, with Mary and John bound for the museum complex in Kensington and the others headed for the market at Notting Hill Gate. It was decided it would be in their best interest if Mr. Sullivan went with the larger group, and John and Mary were left to their own devices, accompanied by a tube map and a day pass. Mr. Sullivan did give them directions, including instructions to follow the tunnel to the museum from the underground station at Gloucester Street, so they didn't have to dodge London traffic.

When the door of the train closed behind Mr. Sullivan and his charges, Mary breathed a sigh of relief. "I don't know what makes me happier. Being left alone by the U.S. Government, or just being left alone."

"I know what you mean. Now then, do you really want to go to the museum, or would you rather just strike out on our own? It's up to you; we'll do whatever you want."

Mary put her arm around John's waist as they headed down one level to get the east-bound train. "What I'd like to do and what we're going to do are two different things, Mr. Finestre. We're going to find someplace to talk where there are no MP's, no escorts and no family members around. I think we need to head over to the park and find a quiet bench and have a long discussion about what we are going to do."

Rather than a park, they went to the Victoria and Albert after all. They sat on the bench in the courtyard and watched the pigeons and sparrows. After just watching the birds and the people in the courtyard for a while, John excused himself and went inside. He emerged moments later with a white paper sack, and two cups of tea. He presented one of the cups to Mary and sat beside her. Opening the bag, John removed a slice of the most wonderful chocolate torte Mary had seen in years.

While they nibbled the cake and sipped their tea, they spoke of nonsensical thinks, such as what they would do tomorrow, and what their respective grandchildren liked to eat. When the cake was consumed and the crumbs fed to the waiting birds, Mary turned to John and said, "How do you intend to answer Harry when you see him again? I know the rest of the family respects you as much as they do Jimmy, and they'll follow your lead."

"I've thought of little else, actually. This is one of those situations I'd just as soon leave to someone else."

"You know very well there is no one else."

"That's the problem. There's no one but us. Given that, I don't think I have a choice. I'll do whatever they ask, if it will help free our country from the oppression of the present administration."

"Are you sure, John? I don't want you to do anything you're not comfortable with. This is really your decision."

"I know that, Mary," he said as he put his arm across the back of the bench. "I haven't been comfortable since the Gingrich administration came into power. Something has to be done, by someone. It might as well be us."

They left the courtyard, and strolled inside. They made

a brief tour of the galleries, marveling at the plaster renditions of the great sculptures of the world. Leaving the museum, they walked the ten blocks back to the hotel.

At John's suggestion, they ordered room service for tea. When it was delivered, they ate the myriad finger sandwiches and sweets, and watched television, which was still a treat for them. When John went in to take a shower to get ready for the meeting that evening with Harry, he was surprised when the shower curtain opened and his wife stepped into join him.

"Well, this is a nice surprise."

"If you want me to leave, I will," she as she ran her hands down his torso. "But you wanted to help me take a shower while we were on the shuttle. I thought, since we had more room now, I'd take you up on it."

Chapter 35

They were both demurely dressed when the rest of the family arrived. John took Jimmy and Neal aside to speak with them privately. When they rejoined the group, it was obvious a decision had been made.

"Ma," Jimmy said, "we've decided we are going to go along with Harry's plans. They may sound a little crazy, but somebody has got to do something, before we've got another Stalin or Hitler on our hands. They way things are going, you know it won't take long."

"I don't think I like the way this is leading," Erin said to Neal.

"I didn't think you would," Neal said as he sat next to her. "We've all talked it over, and we think it best if Jimmy took Sean with him on the shuttle mission. He's already a better pilot than I, and he has a cooler head in emergencies."

"But Neal, he's just turned nineteen! Isn't that a little too young to put something like this on him?"

"No, Erin, I don't think so. But it's up to him. When he gets here, we'll make him the offer and see what he says. Jimmy thinks, and we agree, the Austin should go, too. He's more familiar with the layout and staffing requirements than we are, and if we find we can't trust him, at least we can watch him."

"And you, Mr. Finestre, what will you be doing while your stepson is off gallivanting in space?" Mary asked.

"Other than stay here and keep you happy, Neal and I are going to work with Harry and try to set up the most advantageous method of gaining access to the country."

Harry arrived with Ms. Whittier and Mr. Sullivan in tow. "Ladies, gentleman, it's good to see you again," he said as he took the seat across from Mary and John. "I've made arrangements for us to have dinner in a pub round the corner.

Of course, we've had to rent the entire establishment for the evening so we're not disturbed, but I didn't think that would be a problem. I home no one minds, but occasionally, I get a craving for that incredibly tacky 'pub grub' you can only get with a pint."

"I think that's fine, Harry," Jimmy said. "But before we do anything else, we would like to include Austin, Fiona and Sean in our plans. They're old enough to know what's going on, and this will affect them as well."

"Certainly. Rose, would you be good enough to gather the three in question and meet us in the lobby."

When everyone had gathered in the lobby, Harry led the way towards the waiting limousine. Before he reached the door, he turned to ask, "Is anyone averse to a four block walk to dinner? I believe we can walk it faster than we can ride."

With all in agreement, they made the four blocks in no time. As they rounded the last corner, they saw the quaint building with the small sign declaring "The Rose and Thistle." Above the lintel was the heraldic device of crossed stems of a Tudor rose and a Scots thistle. Inside, banners of tartans festooned the ceiling, while the walls were decorated with pike-staffs, helms and breastplates representing the armorer's trade/ above the bar, instead of the usual mirror, was a collection of swords, from an eating knife from the middle ages to a claymore.

Neal asked the bartender if he could step behind the bar fro a closer look. With the reverence of a priest, he lifted down the claymore with both hands to study it closely. "Jimmy, look at this thing. It's almost as tall as I am, yet it's balanced superbly. Can you imagine carrying something like this into battle?"

"Neal," his wife said, "put that back. You're like a kid in the toy department."

"Beggin' your pardon, sir," the bartender said to Neal,

"wif his Grace's permission, I've a room in the rear with some Viking weaponry you might like. We can 'ave a look later, after you eat."

Neal looked at Harry pleadingly. "That would be fine, Mr. Nash. Feel free to show our guests your treasures after we conclude our business. Now then, may we see the menu your wife has prepared for us tonight."

They took sets around a long table, where pitchers of stout, ale and cider had been placed. Harry played host and offered thoughts on the menu items available to them this evening. It was finally decided they would be served family style, with the foods placed on the table so everyone could serve themselves, without bothering the staff. Mary noticed both Ms. Whittier and Mr. Sullivan had withdrawn.

Platters of roast beef, bangers, boiled potatoes, bowls of vegetables, both plain and in sauce were brought in and placed on the table. When the staff had vacated the room, Harry began the meal by serving himself some of the meat and potatoes and passing the plate to his right. That was the signal for everyone to serve themselves, and they set to their meal with abandon.

In raptures over an unusual creamed vegetable, Erin said, "Harry, if you keep feeding us like this, we'll never go home. What is this unusual vegetable? I don't think I've ever eaten it before, but it reminds me of something."

"It should, Mrs. Mulroney. It's a leek, a member of the onion family. I believe England may be the only place that still grows them, as they've fallen out of favor as they cannot be grown hydroponically."

"So that's why onions and potatoes are so expensive at home. I never really gave it much thought. Do you mean you still grow things in soil here?"

"Yes, we do. You see, while the rest of the world was busy polluting their soil in the 1990's, my father made certain it wasn't done here."

John Said between bites, "I never realized the Prince's Trust was that extensive."

"Oh, yes. Father was very involved in anything of that nature. I believe I was his greatest disappointment, in that I persist in eating meat, and could never get used to the vegetarian meals he so favored."

"Well, Harry," Mary told him, "I think you can be forgiven your carnivorous ways, so long as you continue to do other good works. And I think freeing the world of the Gingrich government would constitute a good work."

Everyone agreed, and set to finishing their meal. When they were done, and the dishes cleared away, Harry asked, "Mr. Finestre, what have you decided? I don't mean to rush you, but time is of the essence in this."

"Harry, we have a few conditions of our own. First, Neal and I stay here with the family. Jimmy wants to take Sean and Austin with him on the shuttle flight. Sean is a better pilot than his father, and Austin knows the layout of the Elder Shuttle better than we." Seeing the looks on the faces of the two young men in question, he added, "We'll go into more detail later, guys. For right now, just think of it as an adventure."

Surprisingly, Harry agreed almost automatically. After a brief moment of thought, he said, "Of course, we never though of that. What about your other son, Mr. Mulroney? What will be his reaction be to being left behind?"

"I don't think he'll even notice," Erin answered for her husband. "Robert is more interested in girls right now than in space ships or saving the world or anything else. I can tell you, Your Grace, it's not easy raising a teenager in a celibate world. Not when he just found out there were two genders. This trip to your country has been a real revelation to him."

Everyone laughed with Erin. When the mirth had died down, Sean asked, "Well, now that it's been decided who is going, do you think you could tell us where we're supposed to go and what we're going to do?"

Jimmy smiled at Sean and said, "Son, how would you and Austin like to help return the United States to the Free World?"

Chapter 36

When everything had been explained in depth to the uninformed, plans were begun. Jimmy, Austin and Sean were to depart to intercept the Elder-Shuttle within the week, with a cargo ship accompanied by a convoy of battle cruisers. In the event they were unable to rendevous with the shuttle prior to its docking with the space station, contingency plans were discussed for direct immediate contact with Skylab 6.

In the meantime, it was decided that the remainder of the party would coordinate with the Home Office regarding the possibility of an invasion of the United States. Other than that, Mary figured she, Johnica and Fiona would do the same thing women had done for millennia: stay home and worry about their men.

When it came time to leave, Harry called for the limousine, claiming he had to go directly to Number Ten, to discuss plans with the Prime Minister. He offered to drop the family off at their hotel, but they declined, claiming they'd rather walk.

Mr. Sullivan and Ms. Whittier accompanied them, until they reached the door of the hotel. Austin whispered something to Neal, who nodded. Turning to Fiona, Austin took her hand and led her away from the lights of the lobby for a brief discussion. When he returned, smiling, he said, "If you will excuse us, Fee and I would like to take a walk before we come in. Is that alright with you, Mrs. Mulroney?"

"Certainly, Austin. But only if you promise to call me Erin. Just don't stay out too late. They lock the lobby doors at midnight."

Jimmy said to John, "Did I just hear him call her 'Fee'? I didn't think she let anyone outside the family get away with that."

"Don't worry, Jimmy. Nothing will happen they're not

ready for," John told him.

"What do you mean, 'not ready for'?"

"Jimmy," Mary said, "John had THE TALK with Austin, as no one else ever has. The same day, Fiona and I had a long discussion, while Erin made sure she knew the mechanics, and the school made certain she never put it to practical experience, it was up to me to go over the intricacies of the actual encounter. We not only discussed how to say 'no,' but when is right to say 'yes'."

Neal laughed and clapped a hand on Jimmy's shoulder. "Jimmy, she MY daughter. I say its about time she actually developed a healthy relationship with a young man. And if she decides to take thing a step further, while I may not be exactly happy about it, I will respect her decision, and honor her wishes. Now back off, Mama Bear."

Jimmy couldn't help but laugh with everyone else. When the laughter died down, he asked, "John, when you said you had THE TALK with Austin, please tell me you covered the need for...ah..."looking around at the women, he suddenly had trouble forming a coherent sentence that wouldn't be offensive.

"Do you mean did I talk about protection and birth control? Not only did we discuss it, but remember when we stopped at Boots on the way to the hotel? I helped him buy prophylactics. They're young, full of raging hormones. If they're going to do something anyway, I at least wanted them to have the option of protection."

This time it was John's turn to receive Neal's hand on his shoulder. "Step-father-in-law, I think that was more than even I needed to know."

Around 12:30, while John and Mary were sitting up in bed, watching reruns of "Euro-trash" from the 1990's, someone knocked on the door. John threw on his robe and went to answer it. When he returned, he said, "Mary, put on your gown and robe, and I'll ring down for some tea. Fiona's back and she wants to talk to you."

Mary did as John said, and met Fiona in the parlor. They hugged before they sat down next to each other on the sofa. Mary asked, "Well, did you have a good time?"

Fiona went into raptures. "Oh, granny, it was the best time I ever had. We rode the omnibus around Piccadilly Circus, and took a hansom cab ride through Hyde Park. I never knew what it was like to spend time alone with a man like that."

The tea arrived, and Mary poured for both of them. John had already excused himself to the other room, sensing this was not the place for a man. While Mary and Fiona talked, John decided he would call Austin on the phone to make sure everything went all right, knowing Austin had no one else in whom he could confide."

Fiona told Mary, "I never knew it could be like that."

Mary almost choked on her tea. "You never knew WHAT could be like that?"

"I didn't know I could have so much fun just walking, sitting and talking to a man. We had a gook time even when we weren't talking. And Granny, when we were taking the cab ride through the park, he even held my hand!"

Mary released the breath she didn't realize she had been holding. For all her brave talk, this was still her baby granddaughter, whose diapers she had changed, and who she'd watch grow up. Sex in theory and in reality, Mary discovered, were two completely different things. "He held your hand, huh?"

"Yes, and then, you know what else he did? When he left me at your door, he kissed me!"

Warming to the topic, Mary had to ask, "He kissed you?"

"Oh, yes." Fiona pointed to her cheek. "Right here. It

still tingles."

Mary laughed lightly. "Fee, you have a treasure in young Austin. He seems like a real gentleman."

"I think so, too. Now," taking the last sip of tea and replacing the cup on the tray, "I think I'm off to bed. It's been a long day and I'm ready to crash."

Bidding each other good night, Mary turned out the lights and returned to the bedroom just as John was hanging up the phone. As soon as he broke the connection, he fell back on the bed in a fit of near-hysterical laughter.

"What on earth is wrong with you?"

When he caught his breath, he took his wife in his arms. "Now I know how those women used to feel who worked for the telephone sex lines."

"What do you mean?"

"You'll never believe this, but I just had to explain both the rudiments and efficacies of masturbation to our granddaughter's date."

Chapter 37

Following the estate agents to the new properties in the limousine designated for their use, Mary was awed by the stately homes they passed. When they finally arrived at their destination, they were just outside the area known as Kensington. The houses were Edwardian in design, looming four stories above street level. They had previously been broken into three apartments each, and were available for sale as the entire row, individual houses or by the flat. Neal was the first to approach the estate agent.

"How many square feet comprise each flat, Mrs. Pettijohn?" He had learned quickly that things were different her than at home when it came to business. Frequently, women were business leaders, as well as in their families.

"It varies, Mr. Mulroney. Each house has a basement flat, with only about seven hundred fifty square feet. Then upstairs, you'll find two flats, of two floors each, with approximately twice the square footage of the basement flats. Of course, it varies according to the layout of each individual unit. With your permission, I would love to would love to show you about."

Following Mrs. Pettijohn, they ventured into the first house through the front door. Inside the foyer were three doors, each leading to a different apartment, with a buzzer for each. Mrs. Pettijohn produced a key and let them into the door on the left. Inside, they found the place still furnished in an eclectic mix of antique and modern furniture of very high quality. The walls were papered in a subdued print, and at the rear of the room was a floor to ceiling alcove enclosed with windows, with wicker furniture arranged around a small table. Passing through to the kitchen, all the modern conveniences were in evidence, with the exception of a refrigerator. Mary asked Mrs. Pettijohn about that.

"Oh, my. I'm ever so sorry," she said, chuckling at her faux pas. "I continue to forget that you are new to our country. You'll find the fridge under the counter. Since, as you know, space is limited in these homes, and people still shop daily to get the best in fresh food, the storage units here are considerably smaller than what you're probably used to."

Reaching down, Mrs. Pettijohn opened a door Mary had originally thought to be a cabinet. Opened, the light came on, and there was a bottle of wine in the door. "We make certain every home has a bottle of wine available should the parties wish to celebrate their purchase of a new home."

They progressed through the rest of the apartment. Upstairs, there were three bedrooms, two baths, and a dressing room off the master suite. The master bedroom held a huge estate bed, swathed in velvet hangings of midnight blue, with gold tassels to hold back the bed curtains. The windows boasted the same drapery, and the carpet was a plush oriental reflecting the same colors. Jimmy had to ask, "Mrs. Pettijohn, are all the apartments furnished in the same manner?"

"No sir. Certainly not. One apartment in each building is furnished, each in a different style, with different color schemes. It was the owner's idea. He thought, and rightly so, the units would sell better if some came with the furnishings. If you like, we can show you the other units now."

They examined each apartment in the house carefully, making comments and asking questions as they went. Finally, John said, "Mrs. Pettijohn, would you please excuse us for a while? I think we need to discuss some things before we go any further."

"Of course, sir. I will wait for you in the car. If you require anything, all you need do is ask."

With the estate agent gone, John gathered the family around. "I don't know how you all feel about living in each other's pocket like this."

Neal said, "I would like to see other houses as well. My suggestion, though, is to take three whole houses. With the money available to us right now, we can pay the entire asking price for two of the buildings, and about half of the third. With housing the way it is, I believe we could keep the furnished units for ourselves, let Fiona and Austin take two of the apartments for themselves, then rent the rest of the units until the kids are ready to take them over themselves. We'd make enough from the rent to pay the mortgage, taxes and still turn a tidy profit."

Jimmy laughed. "Alright, Mr. Businessman, what do we do if we can't rent the other apartments?"

We'll be making enough working at the Home Office, we should be able to handle the payments on a ten year note. And Harry told me yesterday he'd vouchsafe any note we required, so long as it is within our means."

Austin interrupted. "Excuse me, Mr. Mulroney. I told you all I had some funds put by. I think I have enough to pay the difference on the third building. That way, I could take over the upstairs apartment and maybe we could just split the income for the basement flat."

Neal agreed that was a sound plan. "But first," he told them, "before we make any kind of decision, we need to come back in the daylight and look every unit over very carefully."

Everyone agreed that Neal and John would bring the family back tomorrow, while Sean, Jimmy and Austin were at work. They were scheduled to leave in two days, and Jimmy was determined the housing situation would be settled before he left. When they returned to the hotel, Neal and Erin took the literature the estate agent had left, and spent the next few hours going over them. Neal had also picked up several newspapers, so he could review the housing market.

While Neal was doing research and crunching numbers, Jimmy and Johnica were sitting with their two boys, explaining their new living arrangements. The boys were excited about the possibility of having John and Mary nearby, as both wanted to get to know their new grandfather better.

Sean, Fiona, Meghan, Robert and Austin had gathered in Austin's room to discuss the new arrangements as well. Fiona told him she was surprised he had sufficient funds available to him to purchase half of the building.

Austin said, "When my grandmother died, she left her property to me. Since I'm single and was in the military, it didn't do me much good, and I really didn't feel comfortable renting it out. I sold it to someone else in the family. Fortunately, I put the money in an account to which I can still gain access."

Fiona began to look on Austin a little differently, as a man of business, rather than just a nice guy who made her feel good. "How did you manage to do that?" she asked.

"When I sold the property, my cousin, who purchased it by the way, was a banker. He warned me not to trust my funds to investments or American banks. On his advice, I put all my money, all $200,000.00 of it, in Barclay's Bank on Grand Bahama. And, since Barclay's Bank is still Barclay's Bank, I can get the money any time I need it, right here. In fact, right across the street. Okay, so it doesn't pay any interest, being an offshore account. But at least I still have the money, now I can have access to it. So many at home lost everything."

The more Fiona listened to Austin, the more she liked him. She realized her grandmother was right about men: sometimes you get a keeper, and sometimes they're not worth the trouble to shove them off a cliff. But you had to spend time with them to get to know what's under the façade they present to the world. Or like her sister Meghan told her once, "You've got to kiss a lot of frogs to find a prince."

Sean and Robert finally excused themselves and returned to their room. Meghan wanted to leave too, but was uncertain about leaving Austin alone with her sister. Fiona told her, "Meghan, if you want to go on to bed, go ahead. I want to talk to Austin for a little while longer."

Meghan left, leaving the two of them alone. Austin asked, "Are you sure you want to be in my room, Fee? It wouldn't look very good to your parents."

"Alright, then, how about if we go out? We've got at least another three hours before they lock up downstairs. Am I too forward to suggest it? I'd really just like to go out and walk around with you, maybe go to that pub where we ate the other night for a cider."

When they decided, Fiona went to tell her parents they were going out, and would be back to the hotel before the door was locked in the lobby. But even though Fiona kept her promise to be back at the hotel before lockup, it was a very long time before she returned to the room she shared with Meghan.

In the morning, they met for breakfast in the hotel dining room, for a light meal of juice, tea and the requisite cold toast. Mary was the only one who really took to the English people's predilection for cold toasted bread, but at that point, she didn't much care. She had told John the night before that if she had she had to eat one more "Full English," she would swim to France for the chance at a continental breakfast. Needless to say, he acquiesced.

Over breakfast, Erin noticed Austin seemed more openly solicitous towards Fiona. He made certain his seat was next to her's, and Erin saw Fiona's left hand and Austin's right were frequently below the table cloth. Erin smiled and nudged her mother. Mary had noticed too, and nodded and smiled at Erin.

Austin asked, "Neal, how long do you estimate until we can close on the houses on Rosary Avenue?"

"I figure, by the time you all get back from the shuttle mission, we should not only be closed, but moved in as well.

Oh, that reminds me, I want you and Fiona to take some time this afternoon to go shopping for furnishings for your apartment. Since we won't need the majority of the money for the furnished units, you can pretty much have free rein on what you buy. Just remember, though, to allow for the smaller rooms than you're probably used to."

"Austin," Erin said, "last night when Neal and I were looking through the papers for housing prices, I came across some household furniture advertisements. Remind me and I'll give you the papers."

Mary said, "I saw something recently that just amazed me. Did you know you can order upholstered furniture here that comes disassembled, so it can be carried up to the upper stories without hoisting it through the casements? I thought that was the coolest thing I had ever seen."

"Something I noticed while we were shopping," Johnica said, "even though prices here are a little higher than they are at home, things here are made much better. At home, they build obsolescence into a product. So remember when you pick out furniture, really like what you but, because you may be stuck with it fro a really long time."

Waiting for everyone to stop laughing, Austin asked, "Neal, why did you ask Fee to go with me to pick out furniture?"

"Well, I figure since you're a guy, you have very little experience in that sort of thing. And besides, Erin here says you probably have taste similar to mine when it comes to furniture."

Erin smiled at her husband. "That's right, dear. No taste whatsoever."

When breakfast was finished, Jimmy, Sean and Austin left for the military training center north of the city. John and Mary left with Johnica and Neal for the Home Office. When everyone was gone except Fiona and her mother, Erin asked,

"Do you have anything to tell me?"

"Nothing you don't already know," she said, smiling a prim little smile.

"He didn't force you to do anything you didn't want to, did he?"

Fiona just laughed. "No, Mom. If anything, you could say I forced him. I thought he'd never ask for anything other than a kiss. Last night I got tired of waiting. You know, if someone would have told me how wonderful it can be years ago, I don't think I would have waited this long."

"Was it really wonderful for you, dear?"

"Well, not the first couple of times. But the third and fourth, he finally started to get it right."

Now it was Erin's turn to laugh. "Just be glad of his stamina. A lot of men have to take a six hour nap after just once. But FOUR. Did I hear you correctly, though, HE finally started to get it right?"

"Didn't you know? Austin was a virgin, too. At least up until last night. You won't tell Daddy, will you?"

"Fee, I think your father already has figured things out. He only wants what's best for you. The one we have to worry about is your Uncle Jimmy. You always were his favorite, and he's rather protective of you. I hope Sean can intervene."

When Jimmy, Sean and Austin arrived at the training center, they went directly to the locker to change into their flight gear. Turning around, Sean noticed some long scratch marks on Austin's back.

Sean asked, "Hey, Austin, you sit on a cat or something?"

Jimmy turned as well. Suspiciously, he echoed the question. "Yes, Austin, how did you get those?"

"I didn't realize I had any scratches," he said as he

pulled on his jumpsuit.

Not even giving him time to get the thing zipped, Jimmy reached out and punched Austin square in the face. When Austin regained his feet, Jimmy said, "I hope there is an explanation that does not include my niece."

"No, sir, there is not. Last night was the best night of my life. Before you ask me what my intentions are, or call me out, let me say that just as soon as we get back, I intend to ask Fiona to marry me. I hope you will be happy for us."

"I will be exceedingly happy for you. However, you will not marry her when you get back. You will marry her TODAY. What if she's pregnant?"

"I made sure we used protection."

"I don't care what you used. You've taken advantage of an innocent young girl, and you have to make things right."

"Mr. Callahan, I did not take advantage of anyone. This was something we both wanted. But I will gladly marry your niece, any time and any place she will have me."

That settled, Sean made his father apologize for the sucker punch, and sent Austin to the medic for an ice pack. Looking at his hand, Jimmy decided to accompany him, to get something for his knuckles.

When they arrived at the medical suite, the physician's assistant took one look at them and said, "Don't tell me. The young man here fell. You, sir, caught him with your fist. Is that not correct?"

Both men laughed. Jimmy answered, "Almost. This is an old family tradition. When a young man becomes engaged to one of the women in our family, it is the uncle's duty to beat the shit out of the groom. You know, sort of let him know what he's in for."

"Lud, no offense, guv, but I'm glad we're no kin."

Chapter 38

By the time Sean, Austin and Jimmy arrived back at the hotel, Austin was sporting a first class shiner. Opening the door to his room, Jimmy greeted his wife, sister and Erin's daughters. As soon as Fiona got a look at Austin's face, she knew immediately what had happened. After giving Austin a gentle kiss on the cheek, careful to avoid his bruises, she turned on Jimmy.

"James Callahan, I thought Granny raised you better than that. What right do you have to interfere in my life? And who gave you the right to fight my battles for me?" She began punctuating each question with a thump to his chest. "Don't you think I could have defended myself if he tried anything I didn't want?" Fiona continued to gather steam,. By the time she was done, she was yelling at the top of her voice..."and furthermore, don't you ever suppose you can run my life. I am a full grown woman, and I am capable of making my own decisions. If I want help, I'll ask."

The rest of the family had joined them to learn the cause of the commotion. Mary figured it out first. "Fiona, dear..."

"And don't you start, Granny. It's about time I fought my own battles. This is a free country, and an adult in the United Kingdom has certain rights that are denied at home. I'm just taking advantage of those rights.

Mary just smiled and said, "Yes, of course, dear."

"But Fiona," Jimmy finally managed to get out, "Austin has something he wants to ask you."

"What did you do, you big oaf, beat a proposal out of him?"

Austin tried to put his arm around her, but she pulled away. "No, Fee. This is something I meant to do, anyway. Your uncle just gave me a nudge."

"Well, if that's a nudge," John joked to Sean, "I'd hate to see a shove."

Fiona glared daggers at the two of them when Sean laughed.

"And as for you, Mr. Fitzhugh, what makes you think I need to marry you? Just because we had a good time, no more than a good time. An exquisite time last night, that does not meant I want to rush right out and marry out and marry you or anyone else. I hardly know you."

"But, Fee, I love you!"

"And I love you, Austin. But right now is not the time to plan things like this. I want us to be settled in our apartment, first. When she heard Jimmy's indrawn breath, she went on. "That's what I said. Our apartment. I fully intend to live with this man without benefit of matrimony. It's not illegal here. I even called the women's hospital today and made an appointment to see a family planning counselor."

Erin broke in, "Well, now that that's settled, lets all go out and get a bite. I'm sure you guys could use a couple of sandwiches or something. Lets go back to the Rose and Thistle."

They managed to make it to the lift without further incident. Due to the size of the party, they had to use both cars to go downstairs. Just before Austin got on the lift with Fiona, he looked to his left and saw Mary smile and give him a thumbs up.

The shuttle party was scheduled to depart in thirty six hours. The last full day in town, Harry called to warn them they were to appear before the joint houses of Parliament and the EU that afternoon, and to dress accordingly. None of them were to make a speech, but they had been instructed to be prepared to answer questions from the floor, following Ms. Narwahli's address and introduction. Both Ms. Whittier and Mr. Sullivan had spent the morning preparing them for the meeting, giving instructions on to whom one bowed or curtsied, when it was acceptable to shake hands or merely nod in deference.

They arrived in the Bentley limousine just before the Chancellor called the houses to order. They were expected to proceed inside behind the Prime Minister and the Home Secretary. When they arrived in the vestibule, they saw a man, slightly taller than Harry, who bore a striking resemblance to the Home Secretary. After a moment's thought, Mary poked her husband in the ribs and whispered, "Now's the time to remember your training. That man speaking to Ms. Narwahli is the King. I'm not certain, but that woman with him may be the Queen. It's been so long since I've seen her picture though, I can't be sure."

John answered, "Well he appears to heading this way."

Neal said, "Oh my God. Erin, grab the boys and keep them within smacking distance. Sean, no smart remarks out of you."

King William stopped in front of John and Mary. Mary fell into a deep curtsey, having been told that one only showed obeisance to the reigning monarch. William took her hand and raised her to her feet.

"Please, Mrs. Finestre. You do me an honor by being here. All of you, that's enough of that. As I'm sure Harry told you, we don't hold with the formalities must since our grandmother passed on."

Mary took the chance of addressing him directly. "Your Highness, I was so sorry to hear about the passing of your father. It was such a great shock. When we landed, I took it for granted you were still Prince of Wales."

"Thank you, Madam. Now, let me introduce you to the rest of my family. This is my queen, Michaela, and our children, Phillip and Teresa."

"You have beautiful children, Highness," John said to the Queen. He didn't realize she didn't understand English well until her son turned and translated his words into Spanish. Dumbstruck, John turned to Mary.

"You must forgive my husband, Your Highness. He apparently was not aware that the Queen is Spanish, and hasn't mastered your language yet."

At the King's nod, John said, "Yes, sir, my apologies. Given the ages of your children, I took it for granted your lovely wife had been with you for some time."

"Oh, she has, Mr. Finestre. We've been married twelve years now. However, until my father's demise, we lived with her family in Toledo. At the time, it was more convenient to converse in her native tongue than for her to learn English."

Harry broke into the group. "Good afternoon, Wills. *Y buenas tardes, Michaelita mía.* And my favorite niece and nephew. Now, then. If I may break up this meeting, the Chancellor is ready to lead us in. I believe you all know your places, so let us begin."

Taking their places behind the king and his family, the procession began with all the pomp Mary had expected. She was, however, surprised to see the Chancellor of the House of Lords walking backwards. She leaned up to ask Harry, he whispered over his shoulder, "It's so his back is never to the sovereign."

His Highness took his seat on the throne at the end of the chamber, this queen to this left, and the children stood on either side of them. Mary thought it looked as if they were posing for a family portrait. Mary's party filed with the rest of the visiting dignitaries, and took their seats in the first row on the House of Lords' side of the chamber. The Chancellor of the Exchequer stood.

"My Lords, Ladies and gentlemen of the Parliament of Great Britain and the European Union. God Save the King and Our Great Union. Our Prime Minister, Silvestre Narwahli. Madam Narwahli..."

Mary thought the Prime Minister looked beautiful this afternoon. Seated behind Ms. Narwahli, Mary noticed the

Duke of Argyle, holding a small child. She knew it was common for the royal family to bring their children to these meetings, but she didn't know Harry was married.

John leaned over and whispered, "Isn't there a striking resemblance between that sweet little girl on Harry's lap and the Prime Minister?"

Mary smiled at her husband and whispered back, "Welcome to the free world, John. Ain't it grand?"

Chapter 39

The meeting didn't end until nearly midnight. Servants had appeared to take the children to another room that had been prepared for them, lest they disrupt the proceedings. Eventually, after what seemed like endless questions and arguments, decisions had been made and bargains struck.

It was finally decided that, following the success of Jimmy's shuttle mission, an expeditionary force comprised of NATO troops would infiltrate the United States through the Canadian Rockies. It was possible to enter from the northern-most coast without detection, and to head southward into North Dakota. From there, they would be instructed to target command and control centers on military installations, government offices and the media. Without easy access to their propaganda, the government wouldn't be able to control the populace. The NATO troops were to join with small groups of dissidents and foment unrest.

John had previously told Harry, and had reiterated to the joint houses that night, that "America will not be overthrown from foreign shores, but from within." This was the only way to successfully cause upheaval within the Gingrich regime. It wasn't feasible to launch an all-out attack upon the beaches. Not only could it not be successful, but it would take an unnecessary tole on human life. By letting their own countrymen do the work, it was possible to gain allies in the cause as well as their prime objective, which was the ouster of a dictator.

***

The family journeyed north of London, where the Shuttle launch was to take place. With admonitions to be careful, keep your head down, and from Johnica, "Jimmy Callahan, if you get hurt, I'll kill you," they readied their ship for takeoff.

Sean was beside himself with excitement. Dressed in the uniform of a cargo fleet officer, to his mother he looked like a little boy playing dress up. But Sean knew today he was a man. He would be helping other, not by doing some fancy maneuvering of computer data, but actually taking a physical part in the mission.

Just before the door to the ship closed, Austin stepped back onto the platform. He took Fiona in his arms and kissed her hard, in front of God, her family and the entire population of Great Britain. When he finished, above the hoots of the males present, he said, "when I get back, Fiona Mulroney, you and I are going to get married. I don't care what you have to say about it."

This time it was Fiona's turn to kiss him. "Since you put it that way, I'll do it. But I didn't want it to be my uncle's decision, or anyone else's. I wanted it to be you doing the asking."

Laughing, Jimmy made a big show of dragging Austin back into the shuttle. "Fee, I wish you would have waited until we got back to tell him that. Now I'm going to have to secure him to the bulkhead so he doesn't free-float around the cabin."

After the rest of the rescue team had boarded, the door was secured behind them. Mary was the first to notice the presence of two women as part of the special force. When she asked their military escort, he answered, "Of course, Madam. Women do anything they are capable of doing. We don't recognize gender differences any more than ethnic diversity. I'm sure you noticed the black man in the group? His parents are from Jamaica, and he's the best weapons specialist we have. I've heard he can shoot the eye out of a fly at fifty meters."

"Excuse me, Sergeant," Neal asked. "Did I hear you correctly? Did you just say he could SHOOT something? Don't your troops use the electronic neurological arrester?"

"On occasion we do, sir. But under these

circumstances, Major Campbell thought lethal force may be called for, and instructed us to take the necessary measures. Personally, sir, I feel much better about putting a man down with a clean shot, rather than frying his innards."

Mary saw fit to interrupt the conversation. "Neal, dear, would you mind terribly taking everyone back to town, then perhaps to a film? There's a theater near the Notting Hill Gate tube stop showing a film I believe Jimmy's boys wanted to see. I thought I would take your wife, Erin and Fiona with me for a little while."

"Sure, Mary. Alright, guys. Let's all go to the cinema." He gave Erin a farewell kiss, then said to John, "God, I hope they have a license there. As Harry says, I could murder a Guinness about now."

John agreed wholeheartedly, and helped Neal shepherd the younger ones back to the train depot.

As soon as Neal had his group out of sight, Mary made a grand announcement. "We are all going to that little bakery over on High Holborn Street, near Saint Paul's, and indulge in every dessert they make. I don't care if it's cake, ice cream or bugs in chocolate. We just sent our men off into space, and we need comfort food. And we don't need the company of any men who wouldn't understand. We're going to catch the train at Luton, then take the tube over to the City. If we do this right, we'll be totally sick by the end of the day."

Fiona only half heard her grandmother, as she was busy weeping into a handful of tissues. Mary put her arm around her and said, "Just let it go, honey. If you and Austin have any kind of future, you're going to have to learn to act brave in front of him, then as soon as he's gone, cry and scream all you want. That's why we're going to the bakery. Food has a way of soothing the nerves. And if you're worried about getting fat, you can have your Suicide by Chocolate with a diet drink" Mary smiled at Fiona, then wiped her own eyes.

The women managed to tarry long enough so they weren't on the same train with the rest of the family. Leaving the train at St. Pancras Station, they walked through the maze of tunnels and transferred to the Kensington Line. Traveling the short distance between St. Pancras and High Holborn, the whole group began to get silly. Johnica asked Mary if she had any tattoos. When Mary told her "no," Johnica asked if anybody wanted to see her's.

Of course, everyone said they did. Joni rolled back the sleeve, and taking out a tissue, wiped makeup from her upper arm. What appeared was a bracelet of Celtic knots etched into her skin. Mary said, "Joni, that's beautiful. Why do you keep it hidden? Since we've gotten here, I've seen quite a few people showing off skin art."

"When Jimmy took the job with NASA, he was told what was and was not acceptable. Jimmy had to have his removed. You remember, the one he got when he graduated basic training? I wanted to keep mine, so I just cover it up and never go sleeveless."

"Aunt Joni, can I get a closer look at that," Fiona asked.

After a few minutes of examination, Fiona said, "I wish I could do something like that. It's so pretty and feminine."

"Fee," her grandmother asked, "do you want to get something done, or do you want to be a tattooist?"

"Oh, no. I could never learn to do something like that. I'd really like to get one, though.

Erin surprised herself when she said, "Ladies, after we survive Death by Chocolate, what do you say we head over to Earl's Court and get my kid a pretty picture?"

Chapter 40

The women arrived at the sweet shop on High Holborn, and headed directly to the bakery counter. Each opted for something different, Mary chose a chocolate truffle the size and shape of a softball, while the rest had various cakes and fruit tarts. Passing plates back and forth across the table, everyone had a bite of the other's dessert.

When they had sated their taste for chocolate, the group retired across the street to the wine bar. Johnica declared it was a requirement of getting skin are. Mary said the only way she would ever be able to get a tattoo was to have a "snoot full." Erin promptly ordered a second round of wine.

After three glasses of what John Mortimer lovingly called "Chateau Thames Embankment," or cheap red wine, the four headed for the tube stop and Earl's Court. At Erin's insistence, they disembarked at the Gloucester Road station. Walking down Gloucester Road, they passed an off-license shop. Erin and Johnica ran inside, giving Fiona and Mary instructions to continue round the corner towards Earl's Court. Mary and Fiona had just reached the corner with their partners in crime emerged with a bottle of Spumante and one of Irish whiskey. As Erin said, just in case Ma changed her mind.

They met up just as Fiona and Mary were ready to turn the corner to head the final block to the tattoo shop. The artist Johnica had found was on the second floor above a "doner kabob" shop, between a launderette and charity shop. Climbing the stairs, Erin offered her mother the bottle of Irish whiskey. Mary said, "Oh, what the hell," and took a sip. Then she took another. By the time they reached the upper landing, she had taken four or five sips, and her lips were beginning to get numb.

They entered the reception room of the tattoo parlor, and began looking over the various designs displayed on the walls. Fiona called out, "Come look at this one."

She had found a tiny faerie, dressed in diaphanous blue gauze, her wings appearing to flutter behind her. Surrounding her were tiny drops of silver dust. Fiona asked, "Aunt Joni, can they really do that now, with silver. And look at that one. It's got gold in it. I've never seen anything so delicate."

"I don't know, honey. When I got mine done, you could get black, blue, red, green or purple. We'll ask Master Sudwell when he comes out."

Erin said, "Ma, which one do you like?"

Mary looked around some more. "Oh, I don't know. I can't decide between the hummingbird and the gnome."

"Oh, Granny, get the hummingbird. It's so realistic."

"I'm not getting anything, Fee. Joni, honey, see if you can find me a cup, will you? I feel like a tramp drinking fine Irish right out of the bottle. And some ice wouldn't be ill-placed, either."

Johnica rang the buzzer by the door to the inner sanctum of the tattoo artist. A very tall, very tattooed man came out to greet them. "Good afternoon, ladies. What can Master Sudwell help you with?"

"Master Sudwell, this is my daughter, Fiona. I have decided to give her anything she wants as an engagement present. She has decided she would very like that little faerie. And if is at all possible, my mother would very much like a glass of ice to go with the Irish whiskey she's imbibing."

Master Sudwell laughed heartily. "Certainly, ladies. Come into the rear. Young lady, I believe yon faerie maid would look quite fetching on your shoulder, in the front, just to the right of your collar bone. Now then, lets discuss color. Would you like her in blue, or pink or lavender? If none of those will suit, I'm sure I can come up with some green or yellow."

"Oh, lavender, definitely, Master Sudwell. But tell me, can you really do silver faerie dust?"

"Certainly, certainly miss. Would you prefer the silver, the gold or mixed?"

"Aunt Joni, what do you think?"

"Get the silver. It goes so well with your red hair."

"Alright then, Master Sudwell, the lavender faerie with silver dust. How long will it take?"

"Oh, about forty-five minutes or so. We no longer use the same method as you aunt, here, experienced. Now the dyes are loaded into a template and injected *en mass* into the skin. Most of the time is spent loading the template. And I cover the area to be decorated with a procaine gel, so there's no pain at all."

Master Sudwell directed them to take a seat, with Fiona in what resembled an old dentist chair. He left the room and returned momentarily with a tray bearing five glasses filled with ice. "No sense letting this lovely lady have all the Irish tonight. Besides, I've no license, and I've no desire to be arrested tonight for serving on premises. However, if we all have one, it's an entertainment and quite legal. Now, don't worry, miss, I've never botched a design for drinking."

He poured a small portion into each glass. Mary took the bottle and poured herself some more. Master Sudwell spread a small amount of gel on Fiona's shoulder, then went to his workbench and began to load the inks into the template. After about twenty minutes, he held up what appeared to be a picture made of fine dots. Fiona looked at it in wonder. "Oh, Master Sudwell, that's beautiful. Tell me, though, how do you get the outline?"

"After this has had time to work, the black ink is spread round the edge. The pins on the parts to be outlined are slightly larger and allow room for the ink to enter. Guaranteed, you'll not feel a thing."

Carefully placing the template, he positioned it on her right shoulder between the rotator cuff and the collar bone. He pressed the template into her skin and wrapped an elastic bandage under her arm to keep it in place. "Now then ladies, while we wait for this to set, what else can I do for you?"

They chatted easily about different designs and possibilities. Just before Fiona's time was up, Mary took one last sip of her drink and asked, "Master Sudwell, do you still do words as part of your art? I didn't see any sayings on your display in the lobby."

"Of course, dear lady. I can do almost anything you desire."

"Can you also work the words into a design, so they're not quite so obvious?"

"Certainly. What did you have in mind?"

"May I have a paper and pen, sir?" Mary quickly wrote something on the tablet and handed it back to him.

Master Sudwell laughed uproariously. "Madam, may I suggest this as an ankle bracelet, with a Celtic braid of roses and thorns. It will show that which is desired is not easily obtained."

Mary threw her left leg up on the foot of Fiona's chair. "Master Sudwell, you are indeed an artist."

When he turned to see to Fiona's work, Erin leaned over and picked up the paper on which Mary had written her idea. Erin began to laugh so hard she her eyes were watering and she had to drop the paper. Retrieving the sheet, Johnica read it and passed it to Fiona. Both joined Erin in her near-hysteria.

"Granny, John is going to love this."

Written on the paper were two words: Heaven's Above.

Chapter 41

By the time the four women arrived back at the hotel, John and Neal had returned with their flock, and had ordered supper. The first thing Neal noticed was Johnica's tattoo.

"Johnica, when did you get that?" he asked.

"Oh, this old thing? I'd say, oh, around 1998 or so. I was still a senior in high school. It was my eighteenth birthday present to myself."

"But I've known you for twenty years. I never saw it before."

Neal almost swallowed his tongue when Johnica said, "You never saw my pierced nipples, either. That doesn't meat they're not there."

Mary was still feeling good from the amount of Irish she had consumed. She said, "Neal, you should know by now not to ask a loaded question like that." Then as an aside to Johnica, asked, "If they really pierced, I want to see. I may decide to get mine done."

"I was just messing with him, Mary. But if you're into that, I'll take you back to Master Sudwell's."

John decided to interrupt before things got out of hand. "Mary, my love, who is Master Sudwell, and why would you want to see him?"

"Fiona," Mary called out, "come over here and show John what your mom gave you."

Fiona wasn't feeling so badly herself. Striding up to where John sat, she sat next to him and pulled aside the collar of her shirt. John stared for a full minute, then said, "Neal, come look at this. Is this not unparalleled work? I've never seen anything like it."

Neal agreed. "I know. All the time I was in school, I saw my friends getting tattoos. I even went with a few, trying to work up the nerve."

"I know," John said. "When I was in the service, I toyed with the idea of getting one. But I could never get drunk enough. However," casting a glance at Fiona, "that does not appear to have been a problem for our ladies."

"John," Mary told him, "in case you haven't figured it our yet, Master Sudwell is the artist who did that gorgeous work on Fiona's shoulder. He advised us on some other things while we were there as well."

"Mary, does that mean what I think it does?" her husband asked suspiciously.

"You'll just have to find out for yourself, John Finestre." With that, Mary turned and walked into the bedroom, closing the door behind her.

"Well, folks," John told them as he stood up, "I hope you'll excuse us. Neal, please call downstairs and have the food sent to you room. I believe my wife and I need to have a talk."

Erin laughed as she herded everyone out of the room. "By all means, John. You and Ma have a talk. When your done, come and tell me what you think of Master Sudwell's work."

***

by the time John and Mary got to Neal and Erin's room, the meal was finished, the dishes returned to the kitchen and Johnica's boys had gone to bed. Mary had sobered up enough to want something to eat, and had John call down for a couple of extra snacks for the two of them. John looked exhausted, while Mary looked very satisfied with herself.

"Well, Ma, did John have any trouble...with your picture, I mean?"

"No, not with the picture or anything else, thank you. At first, he just marveled at the craftsmanship of the flowers and tracery. Then he got a closer look."

Neal asked, "John, what is she talking about?"

192

"Mary, honey, come show your son-in-law your ankle bracelet."

Sitting next to John on the couch, Mary placed her feet in his lap. Neal studied her ankle for a long time, then exclaimed, "Oh, I see. John found heaven."

***

After John and Mary had their very late supper, plans were made for the next day. Ma," Erin said, "Neal tells me we can close on the houses tomorrow afternoon. He's found a solicitor to assist us and go over the contracts. Because this is a cash transaction, we aren't hampered with the usual approval time."

"How soon can we move in?" Mary asked.

"Well, if we close tomorrow, I figure it will take another day or so to get the deeds registered, since the system here is a little different that back home. But I figure by Monday we should be able to move in."

"Oh my God! Monday! Fiona, Joni, Erin, in the morning, get up early and get dressed. Erin, you get Meghan and Robert up too. We'll need them. We need to shop." When it came to shopping, Mary approached it as guerilla warfare. It was a battle that required planning, perfect timing and killer instincts when it came to bargains.

When Mary and John returned to their room, Mary put on her nightgown and got into bed. She sat up against the headboard, writing on a tablet. When John came to bed, he asked, "What are yo working on this late at night?"

"I'm making a list of what we need to buy tomorrow. It well take a couple of days to get everything sent."

"What do you need to buy? Only Austin's flat is bare. Our flats are furnished."

"I suppose, then you don't object to sleeping in a bed with no sheets? Or standing in the bathroom waiting to drip dry. And I know you won't mind wearing dirty clothes, since there's no washer or dryer anywhere in the house."

John was sufficiently chastised. "Alright, you win. Do you want Neal and me to go with you?"

"Lord, no. As a matter of fact, I told Erin to get Robert up early. Since you and Neal will be busy with Harry in the morning, perhaps you can send him with Joni's other two boys to the zoo or something. This is one place we don't need men."

***

Early the next morning, Mary and her group of guerilla shoppers emerged from the tube station and descended on Oxford High Street. They started at Tasco's on the corner and worked their way up. Mary picked out a wonderful front loading machine that was both a washer and dryer in one. Everyone marveled at how compact it was. Erin asked about the problem of obtaining television licenses, and Johnica found a vacuum cleaner she liked. Paying for their purchases, they moved on to Marks and Spencers, where Fiona picked out bath linens, and everyone else selected bed linens. Since Fiona hadn't found furniture for her home yet, Mary advised that she wait until a little later to get the accouterments.

After the furnished flats were complete, they took the tube to Knightsbridge. First, they visited a china shop that offered seconds and discontinued patterns, for dishes. The kitchen shop down the street provided pots and pans and flat ware, then they found the little furniture store across the street from Harrods, Mary had seen advertised. Once inside, Fiona had a hard time deciding between the overstuffed furniture or the more delicate designs available. Mary told her, "Fee, you're going to be living with a big man. Would he look a little ridiculous sitting on one of those little Hepplewhite chairs?"

"I think I would like that love seat over there, under the front window. Do you think that would go with the club chairs? I can't make a decision like this. I've never even considered buying furniture before."

The salesman approached them. "May I be of help, ladies?"

"My granddaughter is in the process of furnishing her first home, and she isn't sure what to purchase. Is there anything special you would recommend?"

"Well, madam, to young couples, I usually recommend they furnish the bedroom first, then worry about the rest of the house later. To a single woman, I tell her to furnish the kitchen. On which room would you care to concentrate, miss?"

"Why," Fiona laughed, "the bedroom, of course."

By the time they were finished, they had ordered furniture for Fiona's living room, kitchen and bedroom. Along with the purchases they had made at the other stores, the furniture was to be delivered Tuesday morning, with the understanding that if anything was late, the product would be *gratis*. Mary might have looked like a sweet old lady, but she drove a shrewd bargain.

Chapter 42

Monday, Neal and their solicitor finalized the closings on the properties, with Johnica using the power of attorney jimmy had left. Since Fiona wasn't married to Austin yet, Neal executed on his behalf. Neal left strict instructions with the solicitor to have a quitclaim deed ready, to be signed by Austin and Fiona the same time they signed the marriage license.

Since there was a lack of amenities in the flats, even though they were furnished, the family opted to remain in the hotel one more night. Tuesday morning, Mary mustered her forces, with the women designated to the placement of the furniture, and the men to do the carrying. They were waiting on the front steps for the vans by 7:30 that morning. By 8:00, the first van had arrived with Fiona's bedroom set. The delivery men carried everything upstairs, assembled the bed and dressers, then left. Erin and Fiona spent the next hour discussing the best placement of the things. At Neal's urging, they decided to leave things where they were for the time being, and go back outside and wait for more goodies to arrive.

By noon, everything was delivered, and the real work began. At Mary's direction, they went first to hers and John's flat. The bed was made, spare linens stored and the utensils put away in the kitchen. With everyone working together, the whole operation took less than an hour. They moved on to Johnica's and Jimmy's flat, then to Erin's and Neal's. They decided to leave Fiona's for last, and tackle it first thing in the morning.

Johnica and Erin walked to Hart's to get groceries for their first home cooked meal in their adopted country. They marveled at they selection and quality of goods available in a small neighborhood store. "You know, Joni, I could get really spoiled eating like this every day. Fresh meat, fresh vegetables, fresh fruit. And you don't have to worry about the farmer using too many chemicals or the foods being irradiated. And real, fresh bread for every meal! I don't know how to act in a shop here."

"I know. Milk is still sold in glass pints. You can get all the real butter and cream you want, and sugar is available in any form you want. And we're close enough to shop every day."

"Of course," Erin answered, "we'll need to anyway, since we only have those little munchkin refrigerators. But I don't care."

They almost ran home with their treasures, to begin preparation for supper. The family had decided to eat as a group for a while, until everyone got settled in. It would make things easier, while they learned the peculiarities of the kitchen appliances. Mary loved the economy of movement built into the kitchen: everything was within a step or two of the stove. Fiona was fascinated by the corner sink, and both Erin and Johnica were ready to swoon over the windows that opened onto a private garden shared by the three houses.

When dinner was ready, they ate in Mary and John's dining room. While they ate, they talked about plans for tomorrow, and for the future. John asked, "Neal, when do think we should approach Harry about his work for us?"

"I think it ought to be tomorrow, while Mary's busy ordering everyone else around in Fiona's apartment."

Even Mary laughed. "John, instead of going to Harry, why don't you invite him and Ms. Narwahli here, for tea around four?"

"Mary, are you sure that's a good idea. I mean it's up to you, but to entertain the Prime Minister and Home Secretary is reaching rather high, don't you think?"

"No, John, I don't. None of this would have been possible if not for Harry. If he thinks it inappropriate, he'll let you know. Meghan, dear, after you're done, would you put some of your artistic talent to use for your poor old grandmother?"

"Sure, Granny. What do you want me to do?"

"In the secretary desk in the front hall you'll find some blank cards. I'd like for you to pen two invitations for me, for your dad and John to take with them tomorrow."

"Granny, I don't know if I can. I don't have a calligraphy pen."

"Yes you do," Erin said, patting Meghan's knee. "I made certain I picked up pens, nibs, ink and extra paper. And William, I stopped at Waterford's Booksellers and got you some of those books you've been wanting."

William ran around the table like a little boy expecting socks for a present and finding a pony. "You really found Stephen King and Dean Koontz books? I can't believe it. I've only been able to find bits and pieces of them the last few years."

"I know, that's why I was so excited when I found them."

Neal interrupted. "Oh, Meg, William, I forgot to tell you. Tomorrow, Harry wanted to talk to your two, anyway. So it's probably just as well he's coming here."

*****

When Harry arrived,. He had Ms. Narwahli with him, and the little girl that had been in Parliament with them. Harry introduced her as their daughter, Penelope. Before anyone could say anything, Ms. Narwahli volunteered, "Before anyone asks, His Grace has asked me to marry him several times, but I've always said 'no.' I have no desire to be tied to any man. I love him, and I love little Penelope, but I refuse to become chattel."

"I think that is admirable, Madam Prime Minister," Mary said, taking Penelope from her and handing her over to Meghan. Meghan took the little girl into the bedroom, where the younger boys were watching television. Since the boys had never had a little sister to torment, they took great delight in keeping her occupied until they were called to eat. Jamison even risked his collection of Harrods' bears to keep her busy.

Rejoining the others in the living room, Meghan sat with her brother. Harry told her, "Thank you for seeing to Penny. She's a dear child, but she can be a handful at times. Meghan, how old are you and William?"

Puzzled by the sudden change in subject, she said, "Williams twenty-one, and I'm twenty, sir. Why do you ask?"

"Have you taken any classes at university yet?" William has, in science. I wasn't able to go, because of our financial situation."

"Financial situation? I didn't know your family was poverty stricken."

Neal answered for her. "No, we weren't, Harry. But there was no financial aid for college, and we could only pay for one at a time. I told Meg is she still wanted to go when William finished, I'd pay for it."

"Neal, do you intend to retain your U.S. citizenship?"

"I hadn't really thought about it. But I suppose, seeing as how we've bought property and all..."

"The reason I ask, in this country, as in much of the EU, a university education is an entitlement to children of it's citizens. Should you decide to take British papers, these fine young people, as well as Sean and Fiona, before she marries of course, will be entitled to the best we can offer."

Erin said, "Of course, it's up to them, but I think it would be wonderful if Meg could get into school and study art. William wanted to be a doctor for so long, but he had to settle for nursing, since it only requires a four-year degree. We weren't able to cover med school."

"I can't promise a medical school education, William, but if you can pass the test, I don't see where it would present a problem. Where are you in your studies?"

"I'm a junior, sir."

"Tomorrow, with your parent's permission, of course, I'll have you picked up and taken to the testing site for Oxford University." When he saw the excited looks on their faces, he added, "Now don't get carried away. Oxford does the testing for all the Universities in the country. It's just a convenient central location. For instance, if you decide to go into medicine, I would suggest you attend the University of Edinburgh. They have a program that is unsurpassed in Europe, with the exception of the Sorbonne.

"Meg," Harry continued, "what was your standing in school when you graduated?"

"I was in the upper ten percent. Does it make a difference?"

"Possibly. You'll have to pass the academic proficiency test, then you'll take the art test. If you're accepted, as I suspect you will be, you will most likely be assigned to one of the smaller colleges, such as St. Johns. They do the best job with the fine arts. Now then, what say I come round to collect you at eleven?"

"Harry," John asked, "when we first arrived, Sean mentioned attending your military academy. Could that be arranged as well."

Harry chuckled at the question. "John, not only is it possible, it already been done. As soon as Jimmy told me how Sean helped land the shuttle, I decided he was bound for Harrow. Now then, I believe your lovely wife invited us for tea."

After Mary had called the children in for tea, Meg and Robbie shepherded them to Johnica's flat, in order to give the grownups more privacy.

Remaining at the dining table to finish their dessert, John finally asked the question that had plagued them all.

"Harry, what exactly do you have in mind for the rest of us, now that the shuttle mission is underway?"

"I want you and Neal to sit with our infiltration people and go over everything you can recall about security, command and control in your country. As for you women, we need you to discuss the best way to contact and influence the women in your culture. Do you thing you can be ready to start tomorrow?"

"Your Grace," Fiona interrupted, "when do you expect the expeditionary team to return?"

"First, young lady, I have a given name, and I would appreciate if you used it. Too many sycophants and toadies address me by my title, when all they want is a favor or cold, hard cash. Well, now that that's settled, I expect them to return in about three or four weeks, depending on the rendevous location with the Elder Shuttle, and what difficulties they encounter when they reach Skylab 6."

"Will you be requiring Austin and Uncle Jimmy's services when you go across the Atlantic, sir?"

"No, I really don't believe so. That's why it's so important that we receive accurate information now."

"In that case, Harry, I believe I can be ready to start working with your people tomorrow. You see, Mr. Fitzhugh and I plan to marry on his return, and I would like very much if we could have our part of this mission wrapped up so we could spend some time alone."

"Miss Mulroney," Ms. Narwahli said, "I believe I can guarantee your part in this will be completed before Mr. Fitzhugh returns. I also believe Harry can arrange for you to spend your honeymoon away from the city, if you choose. Harry dear, do you think you can arrange for them to have the use of one of the wings of Bellvoir Castle for two or three weeks?"

"You'll have to excuse Silvestre's matchmaking. For

a woman who has no ambitions to wed, she is overly eager to impose the state on others. But of course I can arrange for you to use Bellvoir. Or if you prefer, I can arrange for you to take your holiday at Balmoral. Wills doesn't intend to use it this time of year and certainly not with the upcoming international situation. Just wait until Austin returns, then decide whether you want to stay near London or north to Scotland."

"Thank you so much, Harry, Ms. Narwahli. That is so very thoughtful of you. But back to the business at hand, and I'm sorry I changed the subject, I believe you should make a few changes in your plans on who speaks to the infiltration unit. You see, Meg and I both worked in Civil Service. I worked in Customs and Meg for the Border Patrol. We can pretty much tell you anything you need to know."

"Now, Fee," Mary said, "you might not have known, but your father is rather knowledgeable abounded the working of the banking industry, and John is one of the inventors of the Listening System in place in all our buildings. So you and Meg don't really know everything."

"Well, we might not know *everything*, Granny. But we do know the best way to gen an invasion force into the country."

Chapter 43

Fiona knew she really had everyone's attention now. Harry asked, "How exactly do you propose we get our forces past the coast, then?"

"Before we go any further," Neal said, "I think I'll go rescue Meg from the ankle biters. Since we've brought her into the conversation, I think she needs to have some input."

Erin served seconds on the bread pudding they had prepared for dessert, along with more tea, while Neal went to fetch his daughter. Before Meghan could even sit down, Harry asked, "Meghan, if you wanted to get a large force into the United States, how would you go about it?"

"Well, let's see," she said, accepting a bowl of pudding with bourbon sauce from her mother, "first off, I wouldn't bring them overland. It would seem too obvious. I think the best way would be to enter at Nova Scotia. It's still populated by watermen and farmers. They're pretty much subsistence level there, and the government has never had any success getting a foothold there. So far as I know, some of the populace don't even know the place no longer belongs to Canada. It would be relatively uneventful for a British ship of the line to beg safe harbor."

"But how do you suggest we get them there?"

John spoke up. "Harry, when we went to Docklands, I saw two submarines there on display. I realize you don't actively use them, but couldn't they be recommissioned?"

"Yes, I suppose so. Alright, then, Meg. Say we take a submarine to Nova Scotia. What do we do then? It seems rather unusual to take over a government from an off-shore island."

"From Nova Scotia, your force would take one of the cargo ships that lands on the island, commandeer it and sail down the St. Lawrence Seaway, into the Great Lakes. From there, head into Ohio, then south into Maryland. From Hagerstown, it a very short distance to the Capital."

What makes you think we can get ashore in Ohio? Won't they have troops watching for people leaving the sips?"

"You see, Harry, Fiona answered, "first, there's no need to patrol an area where there's no border. Secondly, the closest civilization in Ohio is a prison colony. No one wants to get in, and the inmates can't get out. There's no guards in the prison, only a few low security staffers."

"Why are there no guards? I thought your country was so security minded."

"There's no need for guards. The prisoners are kept behind electronic fences. If they try to cross the barriers, their security vests send a charge through them. They can't take them off and they can't get out. And nobody cares if they kill each other."

"As a matter of fact," Meghan added, "if you can possibly circumvent the electronic system at the prison, they may well be your best allies. Those men have no love for the government, and would dearly love to see them overthrown."

"Aren't they violent offenders? Would they be safe to deal with?"

"Most of them are political prisoners. Of course, there are those in prison for violent crimes, but most of them are incarcerated for having individual ideas."

"Well, if we do get into the country, and we get to Washington, how do you propose we get into a position to take control?"

John answered again. "My suggestion, Harry, is to act as if everything was normal. There are still tours of federal buildings held every day. If they don't go in uniform, and have identification papers, they can go just about anywhere. The secret is to act as if you belong."

Harry and Silvestre exchanged looks. "Harry," she just

"might work. How long would it take to get things operational on the ships?"

"We should have it done by the time the shuttle mission returns."

"Oh, no," Johnica said firmly. "Jimmy's done his part to this point. I don't want him going again. Not to the States. He's too well known in the government, and it's too dangerous."

"No, no, no. What I had in mind was for whichever one of you was most capable to monitor our actions from the command center in Oxford. I don't see any reason to put you in more danger than absolutely necessary."

They continued to discuss possibilities until Silvestre stood up and announced it was past Penelope's bedtime. Mary went to get the little girl, while John brought jackets. Before he left, Harry asked if it would be acceptable for him to meet with Johnica and her boys tomorrow.

Johnica asked, "Why would you want to see me and both boys? Nothing's happened to Jimmy, has it?"

"No, of course not. I have someone coming in tomorrow to administer tests to Jamie and Robert, to see how far they have progressed according to our academic standards. I'm sure you're aware that your learning system is slightly different here than what they may be used to. Therefore, I not only have testing scheduled, but have arranged for a battery of tutors to get them ready to start school next term. You only decision is whether you want to attend normal school or public school."

"Is it a decision that can wait until their father returns?"

"Yes, certainly. No need to rush. I just wanted them to be ready, no matter where they finally choose."

*****

When the company had departed, and the dishes cleaned up, the family gathered in the living room to discuss the evening's occurrences. Mary asked, "Fiona, why didn't you or Meg ever say anything until tonight? It may have saved a lot of trouble."

"I'm sorry, Granny. I'm just not used to speaking to a man the way that is allowed here. Back home you know how it is. When you're addressed, you may only answer 'yes sir' or 'no sir.' If you ever attempt to express an idea, you are slapped down. Sometimes physically."

Neal came to sit between his two daughters. "Honey, have any of the men you worked with done anything to you like that? Or to you, Meggy? If they did, I'd find a way to pay them back."

"No Daddy. But I've seen it done to other girls. And so has Meg."

"Yes, I have. And one of the border patrol guards I worked with took great delight in forcing himself on some of the women working with the patrol. If they had the nerve to complain to the supervisor, guess who was fired? Fortunately, he considered me too 'fat' for him."

Mary was livid. "Meghan Bernadette Mulroney, you are not fat."

"I know, Granny," Meghan laughed. "But I'm glad he though I was. It spared me his attention. But I know of at least five girls it happened to. One of them killed herself rather than tell her parents he had gotten her pregnant. Can you imagine what must have been going through her head to take her own life?"

"No, I can't. But I can see how someone could be so desperate to escape a situation they would consider it an option, especially considering she would be imprisoned for being pregnant outside of marriage. Believe me, until John showed me a way out, I considered it on the Elder Shuttle. It might not have done me any good, but it would have spoiled the agency's plans, at least."

*****

The next morning, Johnica and Erin took the boys to meet with Harry's proctor. While they were there, Harry was called away. When he returned to the office, he was visibly excited. "Ladies, would you come with me, please. There's a message coming in I want you to hear."

They ran with Harry to the communications room down the hall. There, on the monitor, was Jimmy, giving his report. "...and we successfully rendezvoused with the Shuttle. Only one shot was fired, by Mr. Fitzhugh, in an effort to save several lives. Our mission is complete, sir. Due to complications, we are unable to continue on to the station, but at this point, I don't believe it's necessary."

Harry nudged Johnica to the microphone. At his nod, she depressed the key and spoke to her husband. "Jimmy Callahan, you get your ass home right now. I've got a brand new house all ready, and a new bed all warmed up."

"Joni, honey, is that you? What are you doing there?"

"Jimmy, I brought her in to discuss your boys education. Your call was simply serendipitous."

"Well, Your Grace, serendipity aside, my wife has instructed that I get my ass home. And as I have always been the dutiful husband, I believe I will be landing at Luton in approximately twenty seven hours, thirteen minutes."

Signing off, Harry turned to speak to Johnica again, just in time to see her hurrying out the door with Erin. Erin called back, "Harry, would you mind sending the boys home when they're done? Johnica and I need to go shopping."

As they emerged into the filtered London sunlight, Joni asked, "Why do we need to go shopping?"

"We need to get things for tomorrow's celebratory dinner. I need to pick up some wine. And most of all, I want to go back to see Mrs. George and find that sexy little nightie we saw in the ladies' intimate department."

"Well, I agree about the food and wine, but I personally think the nightie is a waste of money. Knowing your brother, I wouldn't have it on long."

"Oh, its not for you. It's for Austin to give Fiona."

Chapter 44

The next morning, Johnica received a telephone call from the Home Office. Harry had asked Ms. Whittier to call and request the family meet with him at Number Ten several hours before Jimmy, Sean and Austin were scheduled to land.

When they arrived, both Silvestre and Harry were waiting for them. Once everyone was seated, Harry opened the discussion. "The only reason I asked you here was to explain some of what has been happening during the rescue mission. There has been further contact with Commander Callahan. He managed to reach the Elder Shuttle much more rapidly than he anticipated. It seemed NASA had originally planned to make a seven day trip take twelve weeks, in order to lull the passengers into a state of complacence. By the time they were to have reached the station, those people would have done anything asked of them. At least, in the beginning.

"It seems there was a mutiny among the passengers onboard the Elder Shuttle. John, your friend Joel appears to have been the ring-leader. As soon as our craft docked, Major Meirhoff and his cohorts made his move. Jimmy said it was quite exhilarating to see a bunch of senior citizens take on the security staff.

"Fortunately, the only problem that arose came from a young security office Mr. Fitzhugh knew. I believe the man's name was Dakota Westin."

"Harry," Mary asked, "did you say his name WAS Dakota?"

"Yes, I'm afraid so. I believe I told you only one shot was fired. Mr. Fitzhugh fired that shot, in order to keep Mr. Westin from injuring a female passenger. This Mr. Westin was apparently known as a bully, and took delight in terrorizing some of the passengers. Austin informed me the passenger in question was the lady seated with you and Major Meirhoff."

211

"So, my Austin was a hero," Fiona gushed.

"Yes, my dear, he was definitely a hero. As a matter of fact, he will be receiving a commendation when he returns, as will young Sean and Mr. Callahan."

"But, Harry," Johnica asked, "I still don't understand how they got back so quickly."

"Simply because there was no need for them to travel on to Skylab 6. Major Meirhoff and his mutineers volunteered to take the rest of the convoy on to the station. It made more sense to have the actual Elder Shuttle dock with the station. The passengers remained with the ship, and many of them, I believe, wish to actually remain on the station for a while, if things can be straightened out."

"It did seem like a good idea at the time," Mary said. "I guess it took people to louse it up."

Harry requested that the family wait for the return of their men at home, in order to allow a thorough debriefing. He assured them he would not keep them long, and would indeed have them home in time for dinner.

While Erin and Johnica were disappointed they would not get to go to Luton to meet them, Fiona was secretly glad. She wanted time to have another chat with her grandmother, and to make her own preparations. After all, it wasn't every day a girl discovered her fiancé was coming home a hero.

Jimmy brought the shuttle in right on time. He, Sean and Austin were slightly let down that their family wasn't there to greet them, but the situation was quickly explained. When they were on the way home following the debriefing, Austin asked, "Jimmy, do you think anyone would mind if I went upstairs to my own place for a while?" I just need some time alone."

"Sure, I understand. But we might have a hard time keeping my niece away from you."

Austin just smiled and leaned back against the seat.

*****

Fiona figured, after her talk with both her grandmother and aunt, that Austin would appreciate both a hot bath and a quiet dinner, without benefit of her large, boisterous family. She had worked the better part of the afternoon getting a meal together. It was the first time she had really cooked on her own, and was a little nervous he would like what she had prepared. On Mary's advice, she had selected things that could be held without damaging the quality: pot roast, potatoes, onions and carrots, with a green salad. Fiona hadn't bothered with dessert, as she figured they could at least join the family for the cake John had brought home.

Fiona heard the downstairs door open. Listening carefully, she could hear her mother greeting Sean and Aunt Joni chastising Jimmy for causing her to worry. Then the door to her flat opened and Austin stood in the doorway. He tossed his flight bag aside, pushed the door shut with his heel, and opened his arms just in time to catch her to him. Austin didn't put her down until he had pushed the bedroom door shut.

It was almost another two hours before he noticed they had furniture.

By the time they got to supper, it was quite late. Fiona regretted her decision not to provide a sweet for after dinner, as she assumed everyone downstairs had retired for the night. But at this point, she did not care. She had Austin, and that was all she wanted at the time. Along with a good meal, as they were both starving.

She and Austin sat on the couch after dinner, watching late night programming on BBC 2. Turning down the sound, she asked, "Are you ready to tell me what happened up there? Not that I'm complaining, but you seemed like a desperate man when you carried me into the bedroom. It makes me wonder what was going through your mind."

"I'm sorry, Fee. No, let me rephrase that. I'm not sorry

I made love to you. But I am sorry I used you to assuage my own feelings." He buried his face in his hands. "Fee, I killed a man. I looked him right in the eyes, and without a second thought, I pulled the trigger and killed him. And it was someone I knew. I lived with this man during training and onboard the Shuttle. And I pointed a weapon at his head and shot him as if he was a rabid dog."

By now, she could hear the anguish in his voice, and knew he was close to tears. Putting her arms around him, she tried to assure him she loved him, regardless of what he had done. "Austin Fitzhugh, I know you didn't do anything wrong. Harry explained you did what you did save a woman's life. Would you have felt better if she would have died at his hands before you shot him? How do you think I would have felt if it had been you he killed?" She took his face in her hands and made him look at her. "Austin Fitzhugh, you are the man I intend to marry. I love you. I know what you did was right. My grandmother and John know what you did was right. YOU are the only one who questions it. STOP IT! RIGHT NOW!"

Fiona had worked herself into a proper frenzy by the time she was done her speech. Then she noticed Austin had begun to smile at her. "Yes, Ma'am. I'll stop feeling sorry for myself. But it may take me some time to forget what happened. Do you think you could help me?"

"I think I could be convinced. What did you have in mind?"

"Oh, I'll think of something. By the way," he said as he stood and led her towards the bedroom, "you did a fine job with the bedroom furniture. You'll have to show me the rest of the flat tomorrow."

Chapter 45

In the morning, Austin and Fiona surfaced in time to have breakfast with the rest of the family. The women had previously decided they would take at least one meal a day as a group, in order to discuss plans for the day, at least until everything was settled.

As soon as Fiona walked through the front door, she found herself tackled by her youngest brother. "Well," she said, "good morning to you, too, Sean."

"I'm just so glad to see you."

Holding him at arms length, she said, "Austin, where's my brother? The kid you took up with you used to put gum and stick-tights in my hair and ice-cubes in my bedroom slippers. This is a man you've brought back."

"Oh, I think this is the same one, Fee. He did grow up a little on the ride from the shuttle when you picked up Mary and John. He really matured when he was called into action this last time."

Everyone gathered around the table at Mary's summons for breakfast. While they ate, the most recent shuttle mission was discussed. Jimmy said between bites, "Fee, you should have seen Austin here. When we came onboard the shuttle, he took point without being asked, and managed to get us through to the bridge without incident. We docked at lunch time, so the passengers were all in the dining hall. Since the Captain was there as well, we made our way there next, after some of our staff was left in command."

John interrupted, "How did Marc Kavanagh react when you took over?"

"Actually, it was rather surprising, John. He just smiled, shook my hand, and welcomed us aboard. He asked us what we wanted, and I told him we were part of a rescue team."

"What did he say to that?" Mary wanted to know.

"That's the strangest part, Ma. He just smiled and said, 'About damned time somebody did something.' I guess he couldn't figure a way out, and was hoping someone else would do something."

Johnica asked, "Jimmy, who was the casualty?"

"Aunt Joni," Fiona put in, "I'm not real sure Austin wants to talk about this right now."

"No, it's alright, Fiona," Austin said. "I need to do this. Mary, do you remember the guard I was originally assigned to partner with?" Mary nodded that she did. "His name was Dakota Westin. When the Captain surrendered his command, and Major Meirhoff offered to take the Shuttle on to Skylab, Dakota wouldn't have it. He grabbed little Miss Violet, the lady who shared you table, and used her as a shield. He demanded the Captain take us all prisoner, and that we proceed as scheduled. He said he was tired of all the 'old farts taking up his space and breathing his air.' I knew I had to do something. I was standing a little to his left, out of his field of vision, as he was concentrating on Jimmy and the Captain. When I saw he intended to kill Violet, I took the one chance I had. He had to let go of her to use the interrupter. As soon as I saw him step back, I took my shot. That's all."

"Austin," Sean told him, "you make it sound like it's nothing special. None of us would have taken that shot. And figuring you only training with the weapon you carried came in three days before we took off, I'd say that's pretty damned good."

They continued their breakfast, and talked about what happened during the mission. Finally, talk got around to the upcoming invasion. "Sean," Neal said, "you'll be pleased to know your two sisters are going to be instrumental in helping with the overthrow of the United States Government."

Sean laughed. "I always said those two were holy terrors. They terrorized William and me often enough. I guess they're finally getting to put their skills to gook use."

Austin asked, "Fiona, how did you and Meg get selected for this?"

"Oh, don't worry, we're not going anywhere. We just happened to know the best way to get around the government's security system. Especially Meggy, since she worked for the Border Patrol."

Later, after the breakfast things had been washed and put away, and everyone was sitting with their last cup of coffee, the proctor called with the boys' test results. They were behind in language arts, but with diligent work with tutors, they would be up to grade level in either public or normal school by terms' end. It was up to their parents where they were to go.

Johnica and Jimmy decided they would take the boys on tours of both schools, and give them the final say-so. Joni couldn't imagine sending them away to boarding school, but knew the kids would enjoy it, after they got used to the change.
*****

Prime Minister Silvestre Narwahli stood in the War Room of Number Ten, with the Home Secretary and her cabinet ministers. They were discussing the upcoming invasion. The tactics descried by Meghan Callahan were gone over in depth. Ms. Narwahli was aghast when one of her own cabinet members said, "Well, she's only a young girl. What could she possible know about warfare. I say we take the troops straight down the Canadian Rockies from Alaska, and into Washington State. That should get the bastards' attention."

"That's my point, Lord Paterson. We don't WANT to attract their attention. We want to slip in as quietly as possible. At all costs, we must avoid taking life in this conflict. This is to be a bloodless coup. By following the St. Lawrence down into Ohio, then overland to the capital, unless we are exposed near the penal colony, I foresee very little danger until we reach Pennsylvania Avenue."

"I must agree with the Prime Minister." The Earl of Cavendish stood. "I see no need to go into this operation as a bunch of swashbucklers. If it can be done, why not take things over quietly."

Calls of "here, here" went up around the room. The Duke of Argyle stood next. "My lords, ladies, I should like to take a vote at this time, as to whether we adhere to the plan as set forth by our distinguished Prime Minister, or if, as Lord Paterson suggests, we send in bombers and a full attack force."

In the end, Lord Paterson's vote stood alone, with the Home Secretary abstaining, lest he show obvious familiarity. The plan was put into writing and presented to the King for his final approval, and to be brought before the joint Houses of Parliament and the EU, as well as the NATO signatories who were meeting for that purpose.

The final decision was made. The invasion was to take place within the month, with France joining the British forces. The other nations were to be available to step in as soon as the nation's capital was taken. It was estimated the entire operation, not counting the continuing peace-keeping mission, would take three to four weeks, barring any unforeseen circumstances.

Further plans were made, including what was to be done with the members of the U.S. government. One suggestion was that they be sent to the space station, under the control of the elderly who had decided to make it home. While it was deemed a fitting punishment, prison was thought to be kinder.

*****

When Harry broke the news to Mary and John, who in turn related it to the rest of the family, Meghan and Fiona were ecstatic. It was a new experience for them to be taken seriously by someone outside the family. Fiona and Austin decided to go home early and celebrate, which surprised no one.

Mary noticed Meghan looked close to tears when the

door closed after Fiona. "Meg, honey, what's wrong?"

"I feel as if I've lost my sister."

"Don't worry. As soon as the new wears off, she'll be back, just like the old Fiona. And look at it this way, you'll be meeting a nice young man soon, too."

"That's right." Meg brightened visibly. "Sean, William, get your butts out here. You two are taking me out tonight. We're going to those clubs up around Covent Garden."

"Aw, Sis," William begged, coming out of the bedroom, "I was just getting into <u>The Watchers</u>. Why do we have to go now?"

"Because I'm tired of being stuck in the house with a bunch of old fuddy duddies. No offence, Granny. And I want to go out. And you to are going with me."

"But why can't you just go with Sean?"

"Come on, you big dummy," Sean said as he handed his brother a jacket. "Don't you get it? If she goes out with one of us, it looks like a date. If we go as a group, it looks like a group. And maybe we can all meet someone.

Revelation dawned. "Ohhhhhhhhhhhhhhhhhh."

"Right, Will," Meg said, and she and her brothers shared a laugh, "oh. Now get your jacket on and let's get out of here. I want to have some fun before closing time at the pubs, and we have to move to the after hours clubs."

After they were gone, Mary sat beside her husband and said, "Did you happen to have THE TALK with those two as well?"

"No, sweetheart, I didn't. But I don't think Sean needs it. And if William gets lucky, we can only hope his English Rose knows what to do."

"I did see Fiona and Meg talking, and there was a lot of blushing going on between the two of them. I trust Fiona passed on her first hand knowledge to her sister, without going into too many details."

"I hope so, too. Oh, by the way, would you ask Fiona to please move their bed to the other side of the room. One of them kept bumping the headboard against the wall all night. Between that and all the thumping on the ceiling above us, I hardly got any sleep."

Chapter 46

It took the Home Office and the EU ministers two weeks, give or take a day, to assemble troops and ready the submarine for the mission to Nova Scotia. When everything was "good to go," Fiona, John and Meghan were called in to review the set up, as well as be briefed on procedure.

All troops wore mini-cams on their person, so the commanders in London could monitor their progress. It was up to the three expatriates to keep up with the team's progress as they made their way to the capital. While Nova Scotia was a mystery to them, once the troops were on American soil, they would be able to direct them to the places and people they needed to reach.

John kept up with the sea portion, making certain transmissions with the sub were not monitored externally. He was in almost constant contact with the team leader, a Scots Major with a wicked sense of humor. The two of them managed to disrupt the entire communications room at least once a day.

The trip to Nova Scotia took longer than usual, given the necessity of avoiding American detection. Coming in under cover of night, they put ashore in small Zodiacs, with a total force of fifty. Fiona was puzzled at the small number of troops, but Harry assured her they would be more than capable of doing the work at hand. Meghan explained to her sister that the U.S. forces no longer carried high-powered weapons, and relied solely on the Neurological Interrupter, which necessitated coming within ten feet of the target. The British and German made arms were accurate at over one hundred yards, in the right hands, and the soldiers carried both deadly rounds as well as stun-loaded shells, meant to avoid fatal consequences. Orders had been given to avoid casualties on both sides if at all possible, but failure was not an option. In the event one of the team was captured, his home country intended to disavow any knowledge of that person or mission. It was something that was not happening, engineered by people who didn't exist.

The assault team took the first available freighter that entered the port, and disabled most of the crew. A few were left on board who had no special love for the government. At dawn, the freighter made her way through the St. Lawrence, and made port near Cincinnati. Silently, the assault force left the ship, with orders for the crew to head on into the Great Lakes and loose themselves for awhile. Perhaps they could develop engine trouble and communications difficulties as well.

Traveling as surreptitiously as possible, they made their way into the prison colony outside Parma. It was a huge structure, surrounded by an eight foot high fence, with electronic fencing all round. Meghan had explained the lack of security personnel, and it was relatively easy for the mechanical tech to circumvent the security system entirely. Gaining entry was simple from that point on, and when they reached the inner boundaries, the prisoners milling in the yard swarmed towards them. The Major, who had taken the point in the operation, fired a single shot into the air. The reverberation stopped the men dead in their tracks.

"Gentlemen, I am Major Rhys Campbell, of his Royal Majesty's Expeditionary Forces. We are here to give you your freedom, under certain condition. May we discuss our requirements?"

A prisoner who appeared to be the leader stepped to the front. "Why should we do anything you want, Mister. Now that you're here, what's to stop us all from just walking out?"

"Not a thing, sir. Not a thing. However," he called out as the men started to walk towards the perimeter, "I'm here to offer you a chance to obtain some retribution for what the government has done to you. How many of you are here for political crimes?"

All but one man raised his hand. Major Campbell asked, "What was your crime, sir?"

The leader spoke up. "That's Rogers, sir. He's retarded. He was sent here because he couldn't support himself after his parents died. Since there's no family, and there are no homes for the handicapped, this was the only place for him. Most of us tried to protect him as much as we could, but sometimes that guard that comes on at night got to him. That's when he quit talking."

The Major signaled to one of the young marine officers. "Ensign, you are in charge of these men. First, get this security gear off them, then organize them into groups according to skills and knowledge. Meg, are you still with me?"

"Yes, Major. I'm here."

"I know we need to head south east into Hagerstown, but how do you propose we get these men into the city without drawing attention to ourselves?"

"Major, if you go into Parma, you should find a bus yard. Since fuel is at such a premium, they are generally run only on holidays so families can visit. I believe your techs should be able to commandeer several of those busses, and make your way into Baltimore. Actually, I believe it would be best if you would go a little further south, to a little town called Linthicum. There, you can get the Light Rail Line into Baltimore, then catch Amtrak into DC. And may I suggest you have some of your new friends drive for you. Some of them will know the route, without any problem."

"Isn't it a little unusual for an invasion force to use public transport, Meg?"

"Major, can you think of an easier way to get into a fortified city, than to act as if you belong there? There's hundreds of thousands of people who take the train there every week. No one ever questions them about where they're going. If you get off the train then transfer to the subway at the Mall, you'll be within walking distance of both the White House and Congress."

"What do you suggest we do with our weapons?"

"Major Campbell, don't you all have nondescript rucksacks?"

"Why, yes. I wondered why you and Fiona both insisted we carry them. I can understand the need for street clothes instead of uniforms, but we hardly ever carry field packs anymore."

"If you were a commuter on the American rapid transit system you would. Remember, these people commute long distances every day. They carry lunch, sometimes a lap-top computer, a change of clothes, usually a change of shoes. You'll see. Everyone else on the train will have one too. You'll fit right in."

*****

At 7:30 the next morning, three scenic cruiser busses pulled up on the parking lot in Linthicum, at the light rail station. One hundred twenty men emerged from them, and joined the que of the next car. The conductor never noticed the increase in ridership that day, and no one was cognizant of the fact that around fifty of the men rarely spoke, then only among themselves, in whispers. Alighting at the Pennsylvania Station on Charles Street, they all made their way down to the departure are, and waited for the next train to the capital.

The trip into D.C. took a little over an hour, and no one noticed anything out of the ordinary. Once inside the station in Washington, Major Campbell found himself a quiet corner and had his men stand guard. "Meg, we made it. We're heading out now. Any suggestions?"

"Take the subway over to the Mall. Get off with the tourists for the Smithsonian. Stay together, in small groups and no one will be the wiser. Get a couple of the men from the prison to act as guides, and have them give you a guided tour of the city. It doesn't matter if the information is accurate or not, it's all for show. Once you get to Pennsylvania Avenue, head directly to 1600. Go in with the tourists, then slip away a few at a time. The President has mostly done away with his Secret Service protection."

"You mean he no longer has bodyguards?"

"That's right. He believes the populace is so thoroughly indoctrinated, no one dares make a move against him. To a certain extent, he's correct. Now then, when you get to the White House, you'll have to provide documentation to gain access. You were all provided with papers my dad made up, correct?"

"Yes, Meg. We've got them. And he provided enough that the prison escapees could become upstanding members of society as well."

"Wonderful, Major. It might be wise, however, if you left a handful of men outside, just in case. I'd hate to see anything go wrong inside and no one able to get you out."

"Why, Meg, that's extremely thoughtful of you."

"Thank you, Major Campbell."

"And Meg," she could hear the smile in his voice as he spoke, "call me Rhys."

Chapter 47

Meg was right. The force made it without incident into the capital, then on to the White house. The Major's men joined the line for the tour of the president's mansion, and waited patiently in line. While they were waiting, she heard the Major ask, "Meg, won't we have to go through security check points to gain access?"

"No, Major..."

"Rhys."

"No, RHYS, you won't. There are no metal detectors in federal buildings anymore, since there are no guns allowed to the populace. And no one ever gets close enough to the president to do him any harm personally. However, if I understand you correctly, you only need to be in the same room with him to take things in hand."

"That's right. The line's beginning to move. Tell me what we're expected to do."

"Take the tour as if you're a tourist from out of town. The end of the tour is the Oval Office. The President likes to make an appearance there to the public. From the looks of things, you're tour should be comprised of only your own men."

"Just keep an eye on us. Forgive me if I don't answer you when you speak to me. I don't want the docent to think I'm schizophrenic."

Meghan laughed at the Major's attempt to lighten the situation. They all sat back and watched the tour through the mini-cams. Meghan took great delight in making comments to the Major about things they saw on the tour, trying to unsettle his composure. She didn't want to endanger the mission at all, she was only trying to pay him back a little for what he and John had done previously.

When the men reached the Oval Office, the Major was

still amazed when the door opened and the President of the United States walked in. All the tour group, save the docent and two elderly people from the Midwest, were members of the invasion force. Looking about, the Major noted there were only two people with the President. Meg told him one was the Secretary of the Interior, and the other was a security guard. Campbell decided the guard was more for appearance than protection.

After Gingrich gave a short addressed, he asked, "Any questions?"

Meg almost yelled into the microphone, "NOW!"

Major Campbell's hand was the first to go up. As he raised his left hand, he withdrew his weapon from beneath his jacket.

The President said, "Yes sir, you wished to ask a question?"

"Yes, Mr. President." The pistol appeared and was leveled at Gingrich. "My question sir, is would you and your men care to step over and face the wall, or would you prefer I splatter your brains right there behind the desk?"

Like all bullies, Gingrich was quick to acquiesce, but even quicker to whine and threaten retribution. "Men," the Major called to his troops, "secure this piece of refuse, please. And if he doesn't shut up, there's a roll of duct tape in my bag for his mouth. I have to make a call to the men on the perimeter."

Meg congratulated him on his swift action. He contacted the ensign he had left in charge outside, as well as the other men still in the White House. He gave orders they were to head over to the houses of Congress, while he made an attempt to negotiate a rapid surrender.

Rhys Campbell went back to the President, who was now bound with his hands behind his back. He had slid down the wall and was sitting on the floor, sobbing.

Squatting next to him, Campbell said, "Listen here, you sorry piece of shit. I know you like to bully old ladies and force your will on an entire country. Well, that's over. I'm going to give you a choice. You can either surrender your country now, and we will allow you to live, or I will kill you and we will still take over your country. What's it going to be?"

After Gingrich whined some more and made a few idle threats, the Major stood up. "I'm tired of dealing with this slimy little bastard. Finchley."

A young man stepped forward. "Yes, sir."

"Take this...this turd masquerading as a man outside and kill him. I don't want to soil the wall paper in here."

"Yes, sir. Thank you sir." Finchley reached down too lift the president to his feet. Gingrich began to sob like a small child. Finchley seemed joyous about his detail. "Right, then. Come along, boyo. Time to act the man, then."

"Wait. Wait." Gingrich was screaming as he reached the door. "I'll do anything. Just don't kill me. Don't kill me."

"Finchley, bring the coward back. Meg, darlin', please tell me you're recording all this."

"Yes, Rhys. It's taped, both visual and audio. I think this should look very nice on tonight's news."

Following orders, the president made calls to the Speaker of the House and the President of the Senate, and recited the designated terms of the surrender. All elected members of the government were to report to the Mall, where they were to be taken into custody. There was to be no resistance.

It took three hours before they were finished, and able to relax a little. When they were done, the plan was for them to head for the Pentagon, where they could take control of the media through the governmental feeds to the broadcast facilities. Orders had been given to the military that the invasion force was to meet no resistance, and they were to receive full cooperation. Neither Rhys or Meghan could believe the ease with which they had conquered an entire country.

"Meg, the way things are progressing, we should be done here within the week. Another day to get back and file my report. On, oh, say, Saturday, would you like to have dinner with me?"

"You know, Rhys, I've spent quite a bit of time talking to you and advising you, but I don't even know what you look like. Have one of the men turn to face you so I can get a look through the viewer, please."

"Finchley, come over here, please. Miss Mulroney want's you to stand back about ten feet and face me. There. Is that alright, Meg?"

Meg saw a very tall, very distinguished looking man in his middle thirties, with a Ronald Coleman mustache and thick, wavy hair. Fiona leaned over her sister's shoulder and said, "Rhys, this is Fiona. Meghan's rather speechless right now. I'd say it's more than alright."

Epilogue

In the end, it took three months for Major Rhys Campbell to return to the United Kingdom. During his sojourn with the invasion force, he had been responsible for setting up the new interim government and making certain things were running smoothly before he left for home.

He continued to speak with Meghan at least once a day, via his mini-cam hook up, but since there were no more transcontinental telephone cables or Global Internet access, he had never really seen her. But he knew her voice and personality so well, he thought he would recognize her immediately.

The assault team landed at Luton at noon, to be greeted by the men's families and a military band. As soon as the Major emerged from the hatch, he began looking for the woman whose voice had so fascinated him for three months. He knew Jimmy, Sean and Austin from the training center, but hadn't met the rest of the family.

He spotted Jimmy standing on the tarmac, with Austin and two very pretty young women. He figured out right away that the one Austin was all over had to be Fiona. Therefore, logic said the blonde had to be his Meghan.

Like a martin to it's nest, Rhys Campbell made his way through the crowd of well-wishers and reporters. Stopping in front of Meghan, he bowed slightly, removed his campaign beret and said, "Mistress Mulroney, I'd like to introduce myself. I'm Rhys Campbell." Then he grabbed Meghan and kissed her.

When he finally released her, they were both breathing heavily. Austin joked, "Jimmy, it looks as if we'll be needing another flat pretty soon."

Jimmy smiled at his niece and said, "Meg, I know this man has been courting you over the radio for three months, but

I would like it better if you got to know him before he became a permanent fixture like this big lout." He gave Austin a punch on the shoulder.

Inviting Rhys home for dinner with the family, Meg left with her group to give the Major a chance to get settled back in an be debriefed. On the train ride back, Fiona made Austin sit up several rows with Jimmy and Sean, so she could have a private word with her sister.

"Meg, the only thing I can tell you is the same thing Granny told me. Don't let him rush you, and don't do anything you're not ready for."

"But all that aside, Fee, isn't he the best looking thing?"

"Oh, yeah. He could give Austin a run for his money any day. And he's got that super sexy accent. Tell you what, let's wait a couple of months, then trade."

Meghan laughed with her sister. "Oh, no. You've got your own. Let me work on getting mine. Do you think he's a keeper?"

"Well, he's definitely too big to throw back. I think once you get him house broken, he'll do just fine.
*****

Fiona and Austin decided that afternoon to set the wedding two weeks off. Meghan was to be the maid of honor, and John the best man. They asked the rest of the family if anyone minded if they just had a small ceremony. No one objected, so long as there was a party afterward. Meg made plans with Mary and Erin to have the wedding at Kew Gardens, where the flowers were kept up so wonderfully. The ceremony was set for late afternoon, with the reception to follow, at Austin's suggestion, at the Rose and Thistle.

When Rhys arrived for dinner, he carried flowers with him. When he was admitted to the flat, her presented one white carnation each to Mary, Fiona, Erin and Johnica. The bouquet of red carnations he held he handed to Meghan. She detached the card and read it aloud. "To my Meg, who made the war bearable."

"Oh, Rhys, that's just beautiful," Meg said. "But you know, it wasn't really a war. It wasn't even a police action."

"I know. But if I said 'you made the skirmish okay,' wouldn't you think that lacked romance?"

The entire family sat down to eat, with much laughter and chatter. Rhys was included in the invitation to the wedding and reception, and it was decided he would act as Meghan's escort for the party. Travel arrangements were discussed, and a short guest list gone over.

After the meal, Sean and William decided to go out. They invited Meghan and Fiona to go with them, with their dates. Looking at the men, both refused. Austin stood and said, "Rhys, Fiona and I were planning to go out dancing tonight. It's a little awkward for us, as we never danced until we came here. Would you and Meg care to join us?"

Gaining Meg's approval, the two couples left for the clubs, in the opposite directions the brothers had taken.

Gathering in the living room for one final cup of coffee before the dishes were done, Mary opened the conversation she knew was on everyone's mind. "John, you don't think Rhys is too old for Meghan, do you?"

Before he had a chance to respond, Erin cut in. "Ma, I've lived with that child all her life. My only concern is that SHE'S too old for him."

Laughing, the women got up to get the dishes started. While none of them believed in a sexist society, it had long been decided the one who did the best, got the job. All three knew if they let their husbands do the washing up, they'd only have to rewash them later. This way, everyone's feelings were spared.

The men continued to discuss the invasion of the United States, and their decision to remain in England.

Jimmy pretty much summed everything up when he said, "You know John, I can't guarantee my boys will live happily ever after. But, at least here, I can pretty much guarantee they'll live."